The Perfect Player

The Perfect Player

RONNIE P.B. HAWKINS

authorHOUSE®

AuthorHouse™
1663 Liberty Drive
Bloomington, IN 47403
www.authorhouse.com
Phone: 1-800-839-8640

First published by AuthorHouse   09/14/2011

ISBN: 978-1-4634-4777-9 (sc)
ISBN: 978-1-4634-4776-2 (ebk)

Printed in the United States of America

Images by Levon's World of Photography featured model Tina of I.C.H. Entertainment group.

This book is printed on acid-free paper.

They say you will only find true love once in a lifetime, and they also say there is no such thing as a true player. My whole life, all I ever did was make money and adore the company of multiple women.

You see, I wasn't a dog. In fact, I was quite the gentleman, and I was always real with the women I dated, treating them like queens. But I had one problem —too many women. I never took the time to invest in one special woman of my own. I always had to have at least two ladies at a time.

They say everything happens for a reason. But that doesn't mean that reason will be for the best. Love is forever, but time is not. I always said I would find true love, but never did I imagine that it might come with a price. I had it all, or so I thought: money, two lifetime friends, looks, and . . . well, you get the picture. All that changed within a couple of months, but I only needed one night to make the biggest mistake of my life.

Come take a ride with me.

CHAPTER 1

The day started off just like the rest, me waking up jumping fresh, hopping in my fly-ass lady-puller. Yeah, I rode fly! A big-body Benz, baby blue with the hard drop top and powder-white seats, baby! Twenty-inch custom wheels with wood grain inside, too. Made me look sexy. I think I got more sex from driving that car than with my priceless charm!

Naw, but it helped out.

By the way, allow me to introduce myself. I'm Jay, owner and CEO of Ravish Cosmetics, one of the most successful black-owned businesses in the Southeast. Of course, you know every player has his clique, and my clique was my two best friends, Shaw and Curtis. Man, we have been down for twenty years or so. Shaw was owner at this sexy-ass steak house uptown called The Villa. As for Curtis, he was a high-profile defense attorney, and he was pretty good too.

See, on Fridays the boys and I would hook up and hit this grown and sexy spot downtown called Club Bracardee's. Real seductive ambience, big-ass VIP section, velvet seats in all the booths, and waitresses who looked like they fell straight off the runway strip. Man, I loved that spot! Besides, me and my clique were on the list, so you know how that goes.

That night was a bit different, 'cause usually I would pick the fellows up and we would roll out, but as I was about to walk out the door, I got a call from Shaw. "What's up, playboy, you ready?"

I replied, "For sho'! About to head your way now, player."

"Naw, man, I'm picking the crew up tonight. I just bought a brand-new QX56, baby! Big body, black on black!" Shaw screamed with excitement.

"Cool, well, come on, man, 'cause tonight is going to be a good night."

As we pulled up in front of the spot, you could tell all eyes were on us. We always valeted, and we hopped out right at the door so all the ladies and haters could see us. Shaw stood about six foot two, with a low haircut in jet-black waves and such. See, my boys had their styles and I had mine. But like I was saying Shaw had on a black mock-neck shirt with smoke-gray slacks. I guess you could say he was fly.

Now my guy Curtis is around five foot eight, and he had on a nice collared shirt and slacks. Then out steps your boy, six feet tall, dreads hanging to the back, rocking a dirty cream linen suit with a merlot-wine collared shirt and shoes to match, shades on, and everything like that. See, I was flashy, real flashy. In a sense, you could say I was loud with mine because I never had shit as a child. Everything I did was payback to the world.

That night seemed a little different to me for some reason. I mean, we got our usual VIP section, and the flow of the club was the same, but I just couldn't get into it. So I decided to get up and take a stroll through the club. "Fellas, I'm 'bout to step off for a few. Hold it down until I get back," I calmly told my friends.

"Damn, boy, this place knows it can bring out some sexy-ass ladies," I thought to myself as I walked through the spot. I've always been told every player has his day. I guess this was mine. As I made my way towards the restrooms, from afar I saw heaven.

Shit! On the real, I thought I was dreaming. Standing in the doorframe to the restrooms was this chick who stood out like a diamond in the dirt. Damn! She had to be around five foot six, maybe five foot seven, and her skin was a honey brown.

I bet you're saying, "Hell, she sounds like a dime a dozen," but let me finish. She had this reddish-brown hair that came right under her chin in a bob. Her body was the closest you can get to perfect in my book, man. I mean that shit! It didn't take me one minute to scope her out from head to toe, and once I did, everything about her told me she was my weakness—after all these years of being the best and biggest player in the Southeast!

When I finally got close enough to see her face, she had these tight, hazel-green eyes, and her lips were soft pink. Then she had a cute-ass dimple on the right cheek when she smiled. "Uh, listen," I said. "If this is some kind of trick to see how fast you can make me fall in love, it probably took a half a second."

She replied, "Excuse me?"

"Wait, let me start over."

Then I grabbed her by her hand, pulled her toward me, and said, "Sweetness, step out of the walkway. My name is Jay, and you are?"

"Shelly, but what makes you think I'm not with someone?" she said with the cutest smile.

"Well, for one thing, a man usually comes out of the restroom before a woman does. Plus, I saw you from over the way, standing here for at least a minute."

Then she replied, "Okay, Romeo, what's really your angle?"

"I tell you what. I can tell clubs are not really your thing, so what I'm gonna do is offer to buy you a drink, leave you with my number, and pray that you use it. Then we can maybe take a walk and get more acquainted that way. How's that?" I said. I could sense our chemistry.

She replied, "I guess that's cool, player, but I might have wanted to dance and let my hair down for a change. You gonna make me dance by myself?"

Now, normally I would have taken her up on a dance, but for some reason I was trying to be too smooth with myself. I was sure she would call anyway, dance or not, so I smiled, kissed her on the cheek, and walked on. I made a few mistakes that night, but when I look at it with hindsight, that was the biggest.

Well once I came out of the restroom, sure enough, Shelly was getting her groove on. I just smiled. Looked like she was having a good time, so I got back to my team and never mentioned Shelly to the fellas. I don't know if it was because it slipped my mind or because once I got back, Curtis shouted, "Damn, Jay! Man, where you been? We just had a section full of dime pieces, baby!"

I replied, "Well, where they at now? Fuck it, man, y'all go ahead and' do y'all thing, I think I'mma head on in early."

Shaw then responded, "Shit, man, how are you getting home? You forgot you rolled with me."

"It's cool. I'm 'bout to call Tyra to come pick me up."

"Okay, playboy, well, you know we'll have a story or two to tell in the a.m.," Curtis said.

Shaw followed up with, "That's what's up, homie. Just get at us tomorrow."

Like I said, I called Tyra to come and get me. You see, Tyra was kind of my ex-girl, but she and I had an understanding. You know how that goes. I really wasn't in the mood for company, so when Tyra came, I told her to take me on to the crib and she did. She had something she had to tend to of her own, anyway.

CHAPTER 2

I came home, made up a drink, turned off my phone, and just kind of chilled out. I just couldn't keep my mind off Shelly. I ain't trying to brag, but every chick I ever dated was nothing less than a dime. Even so, there was something very intriguing about Shelly. I couldn't stop thinking about the way she made me feel. It was like I knew right then and there that I could spend the rest of my life with that woman, and I'd never had that feeling with anyone! I mean, shit, maybe it was time to slow it down. On that note, I fell fast asleep.

A few days went by, and the fellas and I hooked up for a cookout at Curtis' spot. You know how we do it in the South; we had wings, ribs, leg quarters, burgers, and whatever else you could think of. We had a few other people over as well, but we were all outside tending to the food. Then Shaw said, "Man, I met this chick the other night at the club, that night you left, Jay. Bad as a motherfucker, man. Shaw continued.

"We supposed to be getting up tonight for a few drinks! "Hell, yeah. Jay, you should have saw this girl. Man, she was unbelievable. Just as pure as they come," Curtis added, turning over some burgers on the grill.

Shaw said, "Man, Jay, it was something different about this girl, man. Make a brother want to forget about anything else."

I replied as I was sipping on my drink, "I feel you on that shit!"

They both looked as if they'd just witnessed a murder. At the same time, they screamed, "*What! Aw, shit! Not Jay!*"

I answered, "Naw, man. I'm just saying, man, it's time to slow some of this shit down. I'm tired of treating women like toys. They need more than that, and so do I."

Shaw turned to me and said, "Man, Jay, I still don't know how you let some of the women you meet just blow away in the wind. You know I love you, homie, but you have let some of the finest women God ever gave breath just blow out the window."

I said, "I know, man . . . And, to be honest, I'm a little tired of that shit too, man."

We kind of got quiet. I had a way with words, so what I said had all of our asses thinking for a bit.

Then Shaw's phone rang. "Hello? Aw, hey, boo! I'm hanging out with my boys at a little cookout. Why don't you come by?" Shaw asked the young lady on the phone. I guess she couldn't come, because he walked into the house to finish the conversation. I could tell Shaw had some strong feelings about this woman by the way he smiled when he looked at his phone.

Two minutes later, I got a call. "Hello!" I answered.

To my surprise, I heard this very calm and sexy, "Hey, you . . ." Right then and there, I knew it was her: the chick from the club from a couple nights back. I couldn't remember her name, but as soon as she spoke, I could envision her as if she were standing right in front of me. "Hello! Can you hear me? It's Shelly from the other night," she said as I tried to gather myself.

"What's going on, pretty stranger?"

She sniggled like a sweet princess and replied, "Whatever! What's going on? I was trying to see if I could enjoy your company for a little bit, Mr. Fly Romantic."

I said, "Well, I'm kind of in the middle of some socializing right now."

Shelly laughed, and then responded, "I love how you choose your words, you know that? I wasn't even going to call you; I wish I hadn't, since I got turned down."

Now, what she didn't know was that my heart was beating out of my chest because I couldn't wait to see her, but I wasn't ready for her to know she had me open like that. "Well, I tell you what, give me about an hour and I'll call you. Is that cool, baby?" I said to her with a big smile on my face.

She answered, "Yeah, that's cool, and you better call me too."

"Oh, yeah? Why's that?" I asked.

"'Because I have a surprise for you."

I replied, "Shit, in that case, make it thirty minutes."

She laughed and then said, "You so crazy! It's been a while since I've had a man to make me smile like you do."

The phone got quiet, and I said, "Okay, baby, I'll see you in a little bit."

It's funny, because every move that I made with her felt like a mistake and the right thing to do at the same time. As Shaw and Curtis entertained the guests, I finished my glass of vodka and cranberry juice, and made my mind up to go over to Shelly's.

"Well, fellas, I'm 'bout to head out. I got a little something to get into."

Curtis shouted "Hey, Jay, grab you a plate, man, and don't forget to try them beans I made, homeboy!"

"Cool. I'm gonna catch you cats later!"

So I did what my boy said and grabbed a plate, then got ready to head out. My boy Curtis kept some drink, so I looked in his wine cabinet and got a bottle. "Yo, Curtis! I got a bottle of Moscato out of the cabinet, playboy!" I yelled as I made my way out the door.

"Go 'head, Jay!" he replied as I slammed the door.

Before I called Shelly back to get directions to her place, I went home and took a shower to wash that cookout smell off of me. And, of course, just in case baby girl decided that she couldn't keep her hands off me when I got over. As I got myself ready, I found myself somewhat anxious, like a kid on Christmas. Shit, I had to make me a drink to get back to feeling like me.

Now, I didn't want to do too much for Shelly's ego by over-dressing to make an impression on her. So I decided to put on a soft, canary yellow, French-cuffed shirt, basic blue jeans to complement the shirt, and Kenneth Cole on my feet. Last but not least, I had to put myself in a different class from her past dates by spraying on my favorite panty-wetter fragrance, Prada! Very sexy, baby!

"Okay, let's do the damn thing," I thought. As I was starting up the ride, I dialed Shelly up. Funny as shit, as I was waiting for the phone to ring, music played instead. One of my favorite songs, I must say. It was Avant's "Don't Say No, Just Say Yes."

So she finally answered. "Hello."

I responded, "I like your caller tune."

"Well, thanks! I love me some Avant. Okay, Jay, where are you coming from?"

As I cleared my throat, I explained, "Well, actually, I stay a few streets over from Club Bracardee's."

She excitedly shouted, "Are you serious? So do I. I stay in those lofts on Fifth Avenue called The Shades."

I was trippin' because that was where I stayed. At first I was thinking to myself, "She with the shit? Somebody's playing games." So I asked, "Shelly, how long have you lived there?"

She said, "Well, to be honest, Jay, we haven't had much time to really talk, but I just moved down here about three months ago to take care of my sick grandmamma. She passed about a month ago, so I've been staying at The Shades for around a month."

Now at this time I didn't tell her I stayed there too. I just said, "I know where you at. What's your loft number?"

She says to me, "I'm on the second floor, loft number B16."

Man, now ain't this a bitch? I lived in B17. The way our building was designed, that made us right next door!

CHAPTER 3

That meant I couldn't lie about where I was, what I was doing—shit, I couldn't have a date at my place because she would know about it! I thought maybe I was making a mistake fucking with this chick. I mean, she was bad and all that, but I couldn't be giving up my livelihood. Fuck that!

"Hello? Hello? Jay, are you there?" she asked in a desperate manner.

"Yeah, I'm here!" As I was trying to figure out what the hell was going on, I quickly asked, "What kind of car do you drive, so I'll know I'm where you at?" She told me she was in a black Infinity coupe. Now remember, I was already at her place because we were next-door neighbors. I said her, "Okay, give me about ten minutes, and I'll call you when I get in the parking lot."

As I sat in my car, I had to decide how I was going to handle the situation. All this was new to me: having someone that I dated living in my building, and feeling Shelly like I was. Damn! "Fuck it," I thought. "Whatever, whatever."

I got out of the whip and dialed her up again. "Hello, yeah, Shelly, I'm coming down your hallway now, okay, baby?"

"I'm on my way to the door," she replied.

She peeped through the peephole as I braced myself. I must admit I was somewhat nervous, gripping the bottle of wine that I got from Curtis' collection, wondering how good she would look once she opened the door and how sweet she would smell. "Damn, get it together, Jay," I said to myself.

All of a sudden the door opened. She stood there with a peach tank top and white fitted jeans on. Damn, baby girl body was banging! Her hips poked out just right and her ass looked like two cantaloupes. Wait, I'm not finished! Baby girl had the prettiest feet! Shelly was a dream come true.

"Hey you! Come on in," is what she said, walking back to the living room slowly and seductively. I couldn't keep my eyes off that cute ass of hers, and she knew it, because she turned around with a slight grin on her face and caught me watching. "So what's up, fly guy?"

I answered as she took the wine out of my hand, "Nothing much, just glad the opportunity for us to see one another again has come."

"So am I," she said softly, then grabbed my hand. "I made dinner. We can eat now or just sit and talk for a bit."

As I followed her into the living room, she said. "Shit, I'm really not hungry at the moment, but I would love a glass of that wine."

"That's fine. I think I'll pour me a glass as well."

"So, Jay, do you think we met by an accident or faith?"

I took a sip of my wine, pulled her close to me, and replied, "First of all, you have a very lovely home, and I want to thank you for allowing me over. To answer your question, I'm not really sure. Whatever reason it may be, I'm starting to believe I am a very lucky man right about now."

When I said that to her, I felt this strong force in the room. My heartbeat raced through my body. Damn! I wanted to kiss her on those pretty-ass lips, and I could tell she felt the same because I could see it in her eyes. She smiled as she kept her thoughts to herself.

Shelly took a deep breath and said, "Look, it's a beautiful night, the stars are out. Let's go out on the balcony." Before I could answer, she grabbed me by my wrist and led my outside like a young girl would do on the playground.

Damn, it is nice out here. I said to myself.

Out of nowhere, she kissed me on the cheek and said, "Oops, I forgot the wine," and ran back inside to retrieve it. I took a seat and stared out at the city lights. You could hear the night moving: people, cars, and the wind. Man, that shit was sexy!

Shelly came back outside. "I'm back, baby," she said as she sat right in my lap. We talked about any and everything under the sun as we drank that bottle of wine. I gotta say the night was looking like a success.

Shelly had a slight buzz, so I asked if she wanted to go inside. "Why do you wanna go in the house? You think you gonna' get some coochie?" she asked as she pulled me inside with a tipsy smile on her face. "Ooh, Jay, I wanna dance!"

I'm thinking to myself, "What kinda dancing she talking 'bout?" What I said aloud was, "You sure you wanna dance, baby girl? You seem a little bit tipsy."

Before she could change her mind, she was already looking for a good CD to dance to. "Here is my CD! I've been looking for this for some time now." She got up from the mink carpet, ran to me, and said, "Come on, baby! All shit, here we go."

I was a good dancer anyway, so this was turning into a cool idea. Shit, I needed to have a little fun for a change. The first song that came on was Busta Rhymes, "Respect My Conglomerate". Now we all know Busta got it crunk! Shit, we was getting it in, baby! Shelly had some skills, boy. And you know what they say: about how the dance skills are a reflection of your bedroom skills. The first four or five songs were up tempo, so we started working up a sweat.

"Damn, Jay, you can dance your ass off, boo!" she said.

I came back with, "You ain't half bad yourself, girl. Shit!"

I began to take my shirt off, and you know your boy was cut like a bitch! I had a wife-beater on underneath, so as I slipped my collared shirt off, Shelly ran her hands down my biceps and undressed me with her eyes. To a guy who didn't get pussy on a regular basis, this would have been a dream come true, but I didn't want to move too fast as things were really speeding. I didn't want her to give herself to me like this. I pulled back a bit.

The CD changed tempo and Got to be, by Jagged Edge begun to play. Now for those who don't know, this is a sexy-ass song! As the song played, she looked up at me with those pretty-ass eyes, and they were saying, "Make me feel like a woman, baby."

I slowly rubbed down her back with my fingertips, then embraced her perfectly shaped waistline and led the slow dance. She put her arms around my neck, and we moved to the same rhythm. Our bodies got closer and closer. Our minds began to channel the same frequency.

This was no time to play a gentleman. She wanted me to make this a night to remember. She called my name almost in a whisper, "Jay."

I continued to kiss her like I had everything I owned at stake. I stopped dancing, leaned forward, and gave her another soft kiss as we looked in one another's eyes. I then picked her perfect body up as she wrapped her legs around my waist. We still had each other in a lip-lock. The farthest we got was to the sofa. And from that point on, our lives would change in a way like nothing on this earth.

"Jay, make love to me, baby!" Shelly whispered while kissing in my ear and running her fingers through my hair. I had to do this right, and with a woman like Shelly, she deserved nothing less than total satisfaction.

I peeled her top off and placed her hands above her head. I began kissing her neck and shoulders, then proceeded to suck her pink nipples. Shit, I had all night, so I made sure I used every second of it.

Shelly began to moan and grip the top of the sofa. Then she raised her lower body up slightly as if she was asking me to remove her pants. I waited for a bit and explored her upper body with wet, soft, kisses. As I kissed her around her navel, she placed her hands on the sides of my face and slowly pushed my head down to her bikini line. That was when I removed her pants.

Shelly smiled and said, "I can't believe this is happening."

In my mind, I was thinking, "Well, believe it, 'cause I'm 'bout to wreck shop!"

After I got her pants off, I rubbed her hairs down below with my nose. Boy, I couldn't wait to taste her! I removed her undergarment, and proceeded to kiss her thighs and running my tongue up her inner thigh.

She began to act more anxious for me to put my lips on her lips, if you know what I mean. I kissed down all the way to her ankles and started sucking her toes. She let out a loud, "Ooh, baby, that feels so good! Ooh, you making me so wet!"

At that moment, I rose up and kissed her on her pearl tongue and demonstrated why I'm the best love-maker in the world. She tasted like strawberries. I could have stayed down there all night, but it was time to let her feel me. I rose up, pulled her to the edge of the couch, and inserted my long, hard penis into her. Boy, it was tight, but it felt like it was only meant for me. Shelly began to loosen up as she screamed, "That's it, baby! That's my spot!" I could feel myself going as deep as I could go inside of her.

I turned her over as she got on top. Shelly rode me like a new Mercedes-Benz. Our bodies touched and her sweat ran down my body. Boy, that shit was sexy to me. We basically sexed the night away. As she sat in my lap, riding me, I held her body tight and kissed her. Her juices flowed like a river. Shelly rode me faster and harder, then squealed, "Baby, I'm about to come!"

"Oh, shit, here it comes, baby!"

Shelly shook as she climaxed down my penis. She was exhausted from her satisfaction. Pushing me on my back, she lay on top of me right there on the sofa. I held her in my arms as we both fell asleep right where we lay.

So there it was, Jay and Shelly, the beginning of everything else.

After a few hours, I rolled over and noticed that the sun was rising. I glanced around the room and saw our clothes were all over the floor. I sat up on the sofa and put my head in my hands. Shelly came out from the back of her loft. She wore no makeup and had a black silk bathrobe on.

"Good morning, Jay. I see you have awakened. I was just about to put on some coffee and make some breakfast," Shelly said as she sat in my lap and gave me a kiss on my nose. "You okay, baby?" she asked.

"Yeah, baby, I'm good. I just need to get my ass up. I have a flight to catch at eleven o'clock. Look, baby, why don't you go ahead and make that coffee and breakfast, but we need to talk about a few things so we won't mess this up. I'm feeling you, and you're feeling me too."

Shelly kissed me once again and said, "Go get in the shower, babe. It's only quarter after seven. I'll start breakfast, and when you get out, we can talk about whatever we need to."

I got off the sofa and started toward the bathroom. "Make sure you don't burn us up while I'm taking a shower, now!"

Shelly answered back, "Whatever! I could have been a chef, boo."

"I don't know what you talking about."

She threw a pillow off the sofa at me as I ran in the bathroom. "You better!" Shelly shouted, laughing at my amateur comedy.

I took my shower while she got breakfast made. When I got out, Shelly had a t-shirt and some jogging pants laid out for me out on the sofa. "That's all I had, baby, for you to put on.

It ain't like I got men clothes just lying around.
I put what you had on last night in the washer so
you could have something to wear, baby."

"Thanks, Shelly. You trying to make me think
about making you wifey, ain't it?"

"Damn, did I really just say that shit?" I said
to myself. I grabbed Shelly around her waist,
front the back.

"Move, Jay. I'm trying to cook now." It was
hard for her to concentrate, 'cause I was standing
behind her while she was making pancakes. As I
held her and kissed her on the back of her neck,
she turned and said, "Baby, last night was so
wonderful, but I don't think I'm ready for round
two until after we have our talk. Okay, baby?"

"Okay, baby. Well, how much longer on that
breakfast?" I thought this might not be as hard as
it seemed. I believed things between Shelly and
me would be just fine.

Shelly finished with breakfast, and we both sat and ate at her breakfast counter. "Jay, do you want me to start, or would you like to begin?" I sipped on my coffee, and right when I began to speak, Shelly came out with a deep sigh. "Wait, Jay. Let me go ahead and say what I have to say.

"I don't want to rush anything. For whatever reason, you and I seem to have hit it off from the beginning, but to be honest, Jay, I have a lot of things to sort out in my life. I'm not involved with anyone right now, but I do have a guy friend or two."

"Damn, a friend or two? I ain't got time for no drama now, Shelly!"

She laughed and came over to me. "Baby, believe me, drama is the last thing you have to be concerned about. That's why I'm telling you now that I do have two other guys that I'm acquainted with. I know you have your share of ladies now, Jay."

"Well, honestly, I've had my share in the past. But like you said, I have some things I need to get in order, and being a player is something I'm trying to get unused to."

Shelly grabbed me by my hand and said, "Jay, time will tell us everything we need to know. Like I said before, I need to march to my beat right now. If you and I can be an item, then that's fine with me, but it's got to be when I'm ready, baby. I don't want to put too much on my plate at this time. My space and freedom are very important to me at the moment, and I hope you understand that, Jay."

I laughed. "Well, baby girl, you want to hear a joke?"

"Yeah, tell me a joke, baby."

"Freedom I can give you, but space will be sort of complicated."

"And why is that, Jay?"

"Well, for one thing, we are next-door neighbors."

"You lying, Jay! I knew you got over to my place too fast." Shelly grabbed me and wrestled me to the floor, laughing.

"Ouch! Stop, woman, you gon' hurt my arm!" I screamed as we play-fought on her living-room floor.

I got on top of her and kissed her as I brushed her hair out of her face. "Shelly, one thing is for sure. I won't do anything to hurt you, and I will do all I can to supply you with my armor. Now what's all that stuff you was talking?" I yelled while I tickled her belly.

She laughed and screamed, "Stop, Jay, you gonna make me pee on myself!"

"Yeah, I got you now! Who's the man?" We rolled around, playing on the floor like two people in love.

"You something else, you know, Shelly?" I looked in her eyes and gave her another kiss. "I got to get dressed, boo. I'm headed to LA for a few weeks to go over some things with some advertising companies. I have a few new products on the market, and I need to make sure we get the ball bouncing right away."

"Okay, baby. Man, I'm not sure I can deal with being away from you for a few weeks," Shelly said. She poked her lip out and pouted.

"I know, baby, but this will give you a little room to do you and get some of your eggs in a basket."

"Well, you just make sure you don't get to LA and find one of them supermodels while you there."

"Shit, baby, I like my women real, not plastic. Besides, when I get back, I want to do something real sexy with you, 'cause I know you gon' miss me."

"And you better miss me back! Shit, I miss you already and I ain't even got off the floor yet. Now give me a kiss with them soft-ass lips of yours," Shelly answered.

"I ought to make you wait on these soft-ass lips. Muah!" I kissed Shelly and got off the floor. "I gotta go, baby. Hopefully everything moves along smooth; that way I can get back quick as possible."

CHAPTER 4

Well, things looked like everything was meant to be. I went home, changed up, and called my company driver to pick me up and get me to the airport. I made it on time to catch my flight. As I was boarding, I received a text from Shelly that read, "Remember what I said about LA. Don't be giving my loving away lol. I'm gonna miss u baby call me when u land."

I smiled and got on the plane. It was kinda nice to have someone actually on my mind for a change.

While it was on my brain, I finally caught up with my boy Curtis and told him about Shelly and the previous night. "Damn, Jay! Boy, you got to be the biggest player in the world! Shit, they could make a movie about your ass, pimp."

"Naw, that player shit is over for me, dude."

"Yeah, I feel you, but I'll believe that when I see it. Hey, Jay, have you talked to Shaw? He talking that same shit you talking. Hell, I need to find something to fuck up my head right quick."

"Boy, you crazy. Naw, man, I haven't talked to Shaw. I called, but his phone kept rolling over. Hey, man, I gotta go; we about to take off. I'll hit you cats up when I get to the hotel, player."

"Okay, Jay! Oh, where you staying at, dude?"

"Man, I'll be at the Four Seasons on South Doheny Drive."

"Cool. Well, holla back, Jay."

Shit, man, I loved my boys, and now that I had a lady in my life that had me open, I knew I was the man! I was still a little tired from the previous night, so I couldn't wait to get me a small nap once my flight took off.

A few hours passed. "Sir! You can wake up now."

I awoke to see the flight attendant. "Damn. I wasn't snoring, was I?"

"No, but you were looking so adorable that I almost slipped you my number so I can be a part of your imagination," were the words from Miss Maria, the flight attendant.

"Tell you what, love. Since you're such a talented lady, why don't you entertain me at the bar until I catch my LA flight?" I thought it would be a good idea to keep me busy between my flight connections from Dallas to LA.

"How do you know I'm not still working?"

"Well, for one, I heard you telling the other attendant that you couldn't wait to go to the Cowboys game tomorrow. And I couldn't help but notice your skin tone, and it had Mid-South dime piece written all over it."

"Wow, you are very observant."

"Only when it comes to women, money, and business. Now go clock out or whatever it is you have to do to end your shift. I'll be at the bar by gate nine. My flight doesn't take off for another hour and a half."

"Okay, handsome. Can you wait for ten minutes?"

"Do your thang, baby." I mean, she was a nice girl and I had no attention on getting next to her. She seemed like some good company, and I had time to kill. To be honest, the only female on my mind was Shelly.

Maria and I shared some loaded nachos and had a drink or two. Hell, I wished we had more time to kick it. See, like I said in the beginning, I love women, man. Each and every one of them is special in her own way. I could have chosen to make Maria one of my projects, but I was feeling good about my position with Shelly. Besides, Maria was cool people, so I had no need to play games with this woman.

"Well, Jay, looks like it's time for you to head to LA."

"Yeah, I better get rolling." We both stood up and hugged.

"Jay, lock my number in your phone. I mean, maybe we can be somewhat like friends, you know?"

"That's what's up, baby girl. I come to Dallas pretty often, so . . . Well, be good, baby girl. Next time it's on you, right?"

"Nope, I got you on the third go round!" We both laughed. "Bye, Jay. Have fun."

I turned my last bit of beer up and wiped my face. "Okay," I said to myself, "let me get out of here." Finally it was time to hit LA and get the show on the road. I thought three weeks would be a long time, so I was going to try my best to make it two. Little did I know it would be longer.

Anyway, I made it to the Four Seasons, got checked in, made it to my suite, and flopped right down on my bed. My business wasn't going to start until the next day, so all I had planned was sleep, and that's what I did. All day at that.

After some good sleep, I decided to have a shower, go down to the lobby, do a little paperwork, and have a drink or two. Once I got out of the shower, I wrapped a towel around my waist and began brushing my teeth. Carelessly, I laid my phone on the back of the toilet stool. Next thing I knew, the phone started to vibrate and plunged right in the fucking stool. Damn! Wasn't that a bitch! I reached in the toilet, hoping to save the phone before it was destroyed. Now, I had a business phone, plus I had all my data backed up on my computer, so no sweat, right? But that ended up being a rapid beginning to a wild and intractable six months.

Meanwhile back in Memphis . . .

"Yo, Michelle, this your boy Shaw. I been trying to get up with you ever since that night at the club. Give me a call when you get this message, love."

"Hmmm . . . I guess I should call him back. He seems like a nice guy," Michelle thought. She considered my guy Shaw's attempt to see her quite impressive.

Shaw's phone rang. "Hello."

"Hey, Shaw. It's Michelle from last week."

"Hey, what's going on, sweet lady? I thought you skipped town on me."

"No, nothing like that. I was gonna call you. Listen, Shaw, I don't think . . ."

Shaw interrupted her, using a line from my playbook. "I know this sounds a bit forward, but I been waiting so long for the opportune time for this exact moment. Even if it's just for a moment, if you take this away from me, how you think that's gon' make me feel? Now, in order for this to be a storybook ending, all I need from you is to allow me the honor of treating you to a nice, candlelit dinner, just you and I. What do you say?"

Michelle smiled and accepted Shaw's offer.

"Cool. I know wonderful steak house downtown called The Villa. I can pick you up if you like?"

"Well, I tell you what. How about I meet you there, 'cause I have some things to get squared. Let's say six thirty?"

"Cool. I can swing that. I can meet you in front of the restaurant."

"Okay, sweetie, see you then."

Damn! Now what were the odds of Shaw and me both finding the women that we were willing to trade it all for? I guess this was the part where we grew up.

Shaw had a real sexy evening planned. As you know, he actually owned the steak house that he spoke about to Michelle. So what he did was shut the restaurant down just for her. The restaurant had a real romantic setting anyway, so all he had to do was make sure she liked the food. Shaw arrived at The Villa right around four o'clock to get things just how he wanted.

It had been a long time since Shaw had someone to love, unlike me, who'd never loved anyone. Shaw had a lovely wife and child who were tragically murdered at his uncle's home six years ago during a home invasion. Shaw now lived for a chance to love all over again.

It looked like Michelle was a good pick for him because of the way he spoke of her, the way he embraced in the chance of them being a couple. Sort of the way I felt for Shelly.

Time began to get short as Shaw worked to make this a night to remember. "Damn! I need to call my boy Jay. I can't wait to see this fine-ass woman tonight."

The phone rang, and then Shaw heard, "Hi. I'm sorry I missed your call. Please leave a detailed message and I will get back at you as soon as I can."

"Jay, why you not answering your phone, player? I need some pointers, dude! Remember the chick I told you about from the club? I got her coming by The Villa, boy! Anyway, call me back, cat, soon as you get this message!" Shaw hung up the phone in panic.

Then his phone rang. "Hello?"

"Hey, Shaw, I'm parked right in front of The Villa. But where are you? It's raining out."

"Come to the entrance and I'll be standing there waiting for you."

"Okay, bye." Michelle got out and came to the entrance. Shaw met her right on time.

"Damn, baby. Where are your jacket and umbrella, baby girl?"

"Shit, I thought I had my umbrella in the car."

"Well, at least you didn't get too wet. Before we go inside, close your eyes and give me your hand."

"For what?"

"Just give me your hand. I guess you can keep your eyes open."

Michelle and Shaw entered the dining area, and to her surprise it was very alluring. "Uh, Shaw, why isn't there anyone else in here?"

"Never mind that." Shaw showed Michelle to their table. "Allow me, love," Shaw said as he pulled Michelle's chair out so she could sit.

"Wow, everything is beautiful. How did you manage to get the restaurant all to yourself?"

"Sexy, ain't it? I can't even front on you, sweetness. I own the place."

"Really?" Michelle looked impressed as well as flattered. "You go, boy!"

"Yeah, and I have one more surprise, boo." Shaw nodded his head at the waiter. The waiter returned with the food. "I also prepared the meal. I wasn't sure of your taste, so I started with something small."

"Well, I can tell you now. A sister can get her eat on, and it all looks fantastic!"

Shaw had made shrimp linguine smothered in a sexy-ass garlic sauce for starters. Then, to show off his skills, my boy had hooked up what he called a signature wet steak. Dude was a bad boy in the kitchen, no lie!

Not to get off the subject, but I got my shine on too. See, these are the things that women respect. A woman wants a man with passion and romance—not to mention success, and my team was all of that. That's why we were all good friends.

Now, back to that wet steak. It was a slowly smoked porterhouse, topped in a tangy, sweet, made-from-scratch steak sauce with a mist of lime.

"Wow, Shaw, everything looks so good!"

Shaw took a seat as the two got to know one another. They both ate and laughed in the ambience of The Villa.

Things were looking really good for my boy. As the night got older, Shaw walked Michelle around the restaurant, showing her how things worked and giving her the scoop on the business of entrepreneurship.

"So, Shaw, tell me. What's a man so sweet and successful doing single?"

"Well, my story is kinda difficult. I'm actually a widower."

"Oh. Well, I know that's something hard to talk about, so I won't ask what happened."

"I really don't mind speaking about it. That's if you got time to sit with your boy for a little?"

"I got all night, mister, so speak freely."

Shaw went on to explain his life's path, right up to the point where he was standing, looking into the eyes of the most beautiful woman he had ever shared a moment in the bright moonlight with. Yeah; you see, my guy was falling for this woman, and falling fast.

They carried on for most of the night like a couple in love. Shaw wasn't as vicious as me when it came to getting a woman into bed. He took his time. For one thing, he couldn't quite identify when a woman wanted to make love to him on the first night, like I could. So, really, I wasn't vicious. I just gave women what they didn't want me to ask for, simply because they wanted it to just happen.

That being said, Shaw didn't get any that night, but he did earned the trust of his new lady friend. "Shaw, I really had a wonderful time with you tonight."

"So did I, Michelle, and I hope we can get to see more of each other. There are no strings attached to my feelings for you, baby girl. I'm not even gonna ask, 'cause I know a woman so beautiful, so lovely, and so feminine must have someone to hold her close at night. But at the same time, lady, I also know he can't be taking care of his business, 'cause surely if he was, this moment would not exist." Shaw leaned over and kissed her on the nose, then opened her car door so she could get in.

"Shaw, I really had a great time. Thanks for being a complete gentleman. If you are free tomorrow, maybe we can get together."

"That sounds good with me. Shall I pick you up, or you wanna meet up somewhere?"

"Yeah, let's meet up. How about the riverfront park around three o'clock?"

"That's cool, baby. Just give me a call."

"Okay, I will. Good night, Shaw."

CHAPTER 5

Back to LA . . .

The automated voice on my phone told me, "You have twelve new messages." The first message had been left at 12:41 a.m.

"Jay, don't turn out to be an asshole with me. I know you not that busy that you can't pick up the phone and let me know you still remember me. Anyway, call me when you get off of that bitch, 'cause I know you not alone." And the next ten messages went something like that too. It didn't cross my mind to return the sender's call. Hell, I was too busy trying to handle business. I figured I could deal with the bullshit later. Besides, I was running late as it was to the modeling auditions.

I grabbed my room key and was heading out the door when my room phone rang. Damn, who in the hell was this calling me? Shit!

"Hello! Jay, man, what the hell is going on, player? I've been burning you up, dude." It was Curtis.

"I know, man. I dropped my phone in the fucking toilet, dog!" We both laughed. I'd forgotten that I told him what hotel I was staying at.

"Well, damn, other than that, man, how's everything else going?"

"Shit, man, to be honest, it's been a real good look as far as the business, but it look like I will be here for an extra week, dude."

"Damn!"

"Yeah, I know, man. Anyway, I'm running late, baby boy, so try me back around eight o'clock Memphis time, dude."

"What you gonna do about your phone, pimp?"

"Shit, I called the phone people. They shipped me a new one yesterday, so it should get here tomorrow. I paid for express delivery, but you know how that goes."

"Hell, yeah. Well, go on and do your thang, Jay, and get at me when you can, dude."

"Okay, Curtis. Tell Shaw I said to get at me too, man."

"I will, homie."

From that point on, things got somewhat better. Well, I got my phone on time, and my adventure in LA turned out a winner. Now I had to get my personal life back on point. Going back to Memphis would be a challenge, because I had some things to iron out with my baby Shelly.

I landed in Dallas from LA around three o'clock and had a thirty-minute window until my flight to Memphis. As I waited at my gate, I took a little time to reprogram my new phone from my backup software. Damn, where the hell was Shelly's number? Turned out the last time I'd backed up my settings was before I had her number programmed.

"Well," I thought, "I guess I gotta wait until I get home. After all, we are neighbors. Man, it's been three whole weeks and I haven't done anything to show her I wasn't trying to avoid her." When I thought about it, I realized I could have done a few things to show her that I was thinking of her the whole time, but I hadn't.

As I sat there thinking of a way to make it up to Shelly, the gate agent screamed, "Now boarding flight 2769 from Dallas to Memphis at gate seventeen." That was my flight.

Home sweet home, baby! I got on board and proceeded to my seat. In a way, I was looking forward to seeing my new friend Maria, but I guess she was on another flight or whatever.

Well, everything was everything back in Memphis. My driver was already waiting for me when I got outside of the airport.

"What's up, Kevin?" That was my driver's name.

"Good evening, Mr. Thomas. How was everything?"

"Man, you don't wanna know."

"I heard that. Well, I'm glad you're back in town."

"Thanks. Yo, Kevin, do me a favor. I need to make a few stops before you drive me home."

"No problem, Mr. Thomas. Where to?"

I figured I had to make things right with Shelly, so I stopped downtown for some groceries, wine, and a few karats. Hey, man, nothing against flowers, but I needed a bit more spice to my surprise. So what I decided to do was prepare a sexy dinner, a little wine, and drape Shelly with a nice, heart-shaped diamond necklace. That way, she would always have my heart close to her heart when she needed it to be.

I finally arrived at my crib, and to my surprise, as I was walking down the hallway, there was Shelly looking out the hallway window and talking on the phone. She had just finished working out.

"Hey, baby!" I screamed with extreme happiness.

"Well, if it isn't the player of the year! What's up, Jay! You brand new, ain't it?"

"Baby, look. I know you are highly upset with me. So as make up for taking you for granted, I picked up a few things from the market. I wanna make you dinner, share a bottle of your favorite wine, and make things right. You gon' let me do that baby?"

"Jay, you leave town and I don't hear from you in three whole weeks, and you think a bottle of wine and some food gon' make a difference?"

"Shelly, I dropped my phone in the toilet and lost all my contacts. I had a new phone shipped to me so I could load my contacts into it, but your number wasn't in my backup files. Listen, just let me rekindle what we had, baby. I'm not gonna try and make what I did right, but Shelly, I know I'm in your mix for a reason. And it's not to do you harm, baby. I got a million ways I wanna spoil you. So at this very moment, I'm gonna ask for your forgiveness. I'm about to go inside my spot and shower, come back over to your place, and make this a night we both will remember."

I then leaned forward and kissed Shelly right on her soft-ass lips. I took my thumb and rubbed her on the chin. I looked into those pretty eyes of hers, and had to kiss her once more.

I knew at that point she forgave me, but she wanted to teach me a lesson. I grabbed my bags and started walking to my place, smooth as a motherfucker. "I see you about eight thirty, baby."

Then Shelly screamed, "I got a date tonight!"

"You did what?"

"Yeah, Jay, I have some plans already. And you should have made you some with someone other than me. Thinking I would just jump right into your arms because you came back in town."

"Damn, baby, I said I was sorry. Look, we could go on all night arguing about the past, but why not move on with the future?"

"Bye, Jay. Maybe I'll call you tomorrow."

Shelly walked into her apartment. I stood there wondering what the fuck had just happened.

After an hour or so, I decided to call my team up and head down to Club Bracardee's for some drinks and guy-talk. The way I figured it, if she was going out, I wasn't gonna sit at home all alone like a sucker.

CHAPTER 6

I got dressed, then called up Curtis and told him to call Shaw and meet me at the spot. I got there early simply because when Shelly's guy friend came to pick her up, I didn't want to be at home looking like a duck. I got to Club Bracardee's and decided to sit at the bar. I gave the bartender one of my cards and told him to run a tab.

"Jay, what's up, boy?"

"Curtis, what's up, man?" We gave each other the man hug. You know, shake one hand and pat on the back with the other one.

"Damn, player! Shit got to be fucked up for a boss to be sitting at the bar!"

"Man, some bullshit with the new little honey I told you cats about."

"See, already, Jay! I know what the problem is, Jay. You ain't meant to be falling for a woman. Man, you a true player!"

"Yeah, you right, believe that!" We toasted a shot of that silver. "Curtis, where is my boy Shaw?"

"Shit, man, he got a date tonight." Aw, okay. With that chick you both were telling me about?"

"Hell, yeah. Jay, she a bad motherfucker too! Look like a chick you might fuck around with."

I heard that. "Well, it has to be something to her, if he passed on a night with the fellas."

I ended up telling Curtis all about Shelly so he could get caught up on why this shit was affecting me like it was.

"Shit, Jay, you a bad boy, though judging by what I hear, you can fix that shit. To be honest, she sounds like she's well worth it."

I looked at Curtis, and at that moment he made more sense than my whole life had for the last month. And he was right too. Shelly was worth everything a man would want to risk for her heart.

We talked for another hour and a half. By that time Curtis was too drunk to drive, so I got him a cab. The club owner was cool with us—like I told you in the beginning, we were on the VIP list—so he let Curtis park his ride in the garage underneath the club until he came back to get it.

It had to be somewhere between one thirty or close to two when I got home. I staggered my way down the hallway to my spot. I knew Shelly was home because I had seen her car out front, so in-case we saw each other, I was planning on being an ass about things.

Then as I was about go inside the spot, Shelly comes came out her loft with the kitchen trash. "Hey Jay."

"What's up, baby? It's kinda late to be taking out the trash, don't you think?"

"Don't worry about me. The question is, what are you doing coming in sloppy drunk at this hour?"

"Baby, the intoxication I got is a twenty-four-hour buzz from the sight of your beautiful self."

She smiled. I got close to her body, right in her doorway. All I could think about was making love to this woman like I was getting paid for it. "Let me get that trash for you. Come here, Shelly." I took my hand and raised her chin up so I could look into her eyes. "I missed you, baby, missed you like a motherfucker. Shelly, you got me open, baby! What you got to understand is I'm a man before anything else. So before you put me in a class with all the other cats you have dated, realize what I'm saying. You are my central nervous system, and I wouldn't be able to function without you. That's your role in my life right now."

Shelly took a step back inside her doorway. I dropped that fucking bag of trash, and we started kissing before we could make it to the living room.

She had her arms around my neck, and I picked her up by that soft, sweet ass of hers as she wrapped her legs around my waist. This time I wanted to explore her body in an unconventional way. So I walked her into her bedroom and we took off our clothes. She started toward the bed, but I grabbed her by the hand and said, "Let's get in the shower."

Shelly had no objections. The water was warm enough to make a steam on all the mirrors and the shower doors. We kissed passionately as I held her against the shower walls. The water ran down my back while I gently nibbled on her pink nipples. Shelly moaned as she anticipated my kisses to cover her entire golden body. Damn! Boy, I gotta say, there's two things I know better than anything: what's inside my pockets, and how to make love to a woman. It's just like being hungry and having the chance to eat your favorite food to conquer your appetite.

In other words, I wanted to worship her body. I could feel her pulse speed up when I was touching and kissing in the right places. I then began to kiss and lick down her torso. As I got on my knees, I started to rub down her thighs with the tips of my fingers. That shit drives a woman crazy, boy!

"Damn, Jay, you making me feel so good, baby," Shelly said. She took her left leg and put it over my shoulder, allowing me to kiss her sweet little kitty cat. I took my time kissing it too. "Jay, I want to feel you, baby!" I got up and went inside her with her legs in my arms like a true Mandingo! I got so deep inside her that she began to hold me by the chest so I couldn't go all the way inside her. We caressed and sexed the night away.

I know we went at least an hour in the shower. We must have ended up in the bed, though, because that's where we awoke.

CHAPTER 7

Shelly rolled over on top of me and asked, "You have a flight to catch today like you did the last time, Jay?"

"Shit, baby, I'm already sky high without catching a flight."

"Is that right?"

"Damn right! You ready for another ride on my rocket?"

"You so silly, Jay." Shelly kissed me and got out the bed. "Let's take a shower, then I'll make you some breakfast."

Sounded good to me, so we took a shower. "Hey, baby, I'm in the mood to do something crazy."

"Like what, Jay?"

"Give me my keys over there. I'm about to run to my apartment and get some clothes."

"What's so crazy about that?"

"I'm about to go out there with no clothes on."

"Ooh, Jay, you best not. I dare you to!"

"Shit, why would I be ashamed? Shit, I'm straight down there."

Shelly laughed her ass off. "That's right, baby! You definitely all good down there!"

I walked out the door naked. Shelly screamed, "Jay, you best not! Shelly laughed and I did what

I said I would. See, man, I did whatever I wanted to do in life. Hell, who dared judge me but God?

This is also a part of me that many women adored, me being sure of myself and seeming calm and smooth about anything, which made them feel safe around me.

Anyway, Shelly and I ate breakfast and watched a little TV, but I wasn't the couch potato type, so we got out and did some shopping. On the way back from the mall, Shelly got a phone call. I could tell it was a man, but hey, I knew from the jump she had a friend or two. The thing was, I also knew they didn't have her interest like I did.

Shelly hung the phone up, and to my surprise, she looked as if she thought being with me was a second option. "Jay, there's something I have to tell you, babe."

"You do?"

"Yeah. Well, I'm . . ."

"Listen, baby, as long as you not about to tell me you used to be a man . . ."

Shelly laughed like she was relieved. "Jay, I don't know what to do with you. Baby, I wish you hadn't gone to LA."

"Why, baby? What happen while I was away?"

"Jay, you know I had a few friends before you came along, right?"

"Look, Shelly, let's not make everything a life or death situation, okay? One thing that we have between us is honesty. I feel you haven't lied to me, and I know I haven't lied to you, so it's all good, baby. What's up?"

"Well, baby, when you wouldn't answer your phone nor return my voice mails, I thought you were avoiding me to spend time with a fling of some sort. And so I wouldn't be the fool, I spent some time with someone that I kinda like, baby.

I haven't slept with him, but we have gotten real close, Jay."

"So you said that to say what, Shelly?" a lot of things had taken place since our acquaintance. I had my thirty fifth birthday back in September; hell Christmas had even come and gone. Here it was New Year's Eve and I was about to miss another special occasion with Shelly.

"Jay, he wanted me to be with him tonight. He's hosting a party, and he wants me to meet his friends."

"Was that him that just called, Shelly?"

"Yeah, that was him. I told him I would be there, and to be honest, Jay, I want to go."

By this time we were pulling up at The Shades. "Well, baby, I don't handcuff women, and I'm not the jealous type."

Shelly popped the trunk of her coupe, and I helped her with her shopping bags. "Baby, go to his party and have a good time. But after tonight,

I feel like you should have a sense of who you are feeling the most." We kissed, and Shelly went inside her place and I went inside mine.

You see, I loved me some South Beach Miami. Even though flying down there with Shelly was out of the question, I was about to make plans to bring in my new year in the sexiest city in the United States.

Right as I began to settle in and make plans, I got a phone call. "Hello?"

"Jay, what's up, boy?"

"Shaw, what it do, player?"

"Man, nothing much, home boy. What kind of plans you got for tonight?"

"Who, me? Shit, pimp, I was about to get something set up down in South Beach."

"Man, you go to South Beach five or six times a year. Come fuck with your boy, dude. I'm throwing a party at my spot. Curtis gon' be there, plus I want you to meet my little lady, Jay."

"You know what, Shaw? That sounds like a winner to me. Man, we ain't kicked it in a minute." Shit, Shelly was hanging out with her new friend for the holiday, so I figured I might as well hang out with my old friends, my true friends at that. "Shaw, what time you want me to make it over?"

"Shit, do it how you do it, Jay. You know how we get it in, baby!"

"Hell, yeah, baby, and you know this player!"

Well, the stage was set. Me and my boys were about to bring another year in together, feeling good, looking good, and living good. I wanted to do as much as I could to enjoy myself without Shelly. Although we were on good terms and everything like that, I couldn't help but wonder, you know? So being around the fellas would take some sting off of me thinking about her.

I knew she would be thinking of me as well. You couldn't have the chemistry we had and not feel obligated to that person. I was pretty sure I had done enough to move up to be her number one, if I wasn't that already. I've never been an insecure guy, but I was moving away from the thought of sharing her time with someone else.

As the festivities got closer, I got my fly together and made a call to Buster's Liquor. One thing about Shaw is that he can throw a hell of a party. I figured he'd have several guests, so I reserved a case of Salon 1995 to help set the party right. I left the crib around eight o'clock, I guess.

I noticed that wherever Shelly was headed, she had already left. In a way, I hoped she would have a hell date and call me to the rescue. I know that sounds cheap, but the truth is, I couldn't help but feel like I would see her before the night was out.

My boy Curtis called to see if it was cool for him to roll with me to the party. I could tell that it was gonna be a good look that night.

CHAPTER 8

As Curtis and I pulled up at Shaw's spot, it was cars everywhere! "Damn, Jay, this motherfucker packed! I know I will find me a dime piece in here tonight!" Curtis screamed.

We gave each other a dap and got out of the whip. "Hey, Curtis, grab that champagne out the trunk for me, guy."

"Woo, Jay, you bought some of that good shit, boy."

"Yeah, I wanted to make sure that we get somebody tipsy enough to sleep with your ass!"

We both laughed as I rang the doorbell. Shaw came to the door. "Aw, shit, here is my crew! Come in, fellas, y'all know what to do."

Curtis asked as soon as we stepped in the kitchen, "Shaw, where is that fine-ass lady of yours? I told Jay she looks like one of his type."

"Yeah, Jay, y'all go ahead and set the liquor down and follow me." Shaw led us into the main party area of the house. "Jay, let me introduce my lady to you, homie." Shaw screamed into the next room for his lady to come and meet me. "Hey, Michelle, come in here, baby. I want you to meet somebody."

At that moment, things went into slow motion. Out of the next room came the love of my best friend's life. "Michelle, I want you to meet my guy Jay. Jay, this is my baby Michelle."

My legs felt paralyzed from the waist down. She flicked her bob from over her left eye and extended her hand to shake mine, looking up at me.

Michelle was the most beautiful woman I've ever seen. The kind of woman I would never forget. The kind I would trade my lifestyle as a player for in a heartbeat. I felt like dying right at that moment, for the woman Shaw couldn't wait for me to meet was my own. There, standing in my best friend's home, carrying the title of his woman, was none other than Shelly.

She held my hand, and I could tell she was in as much shock as I was. Me being the guy who never panics, this was the most difficult situation I had ever been in. I mean, you see shit like this in the movies, but never can you even guess it would happen to you.

I had to do something, so I calmly and painfully shook Shelly's hand and said, "It's my pleasure. I can't believe Shaw kept you a secret from me all this time."

"Well, now that everybody knows everybody, let's get this party started, baby!" Shaw screamed in joy and excitement.

I walked into the crowd of people as the music played loud, and Curtis followed. "Jay, what's up, man? You went from ready to get crunk to 'I wish I never met her.' What in the hell is up, dog?"

I turned to Curtis and said, "Everything is everything, baby! Go find that dime you gon' get drunk and spend the night with."

"Damn right! Shit, Jay, I'm 'bout to go get me something else to drank, you want something?"

"Yeah, bring me whatever you get."

"Okay. You sure you good, Jay?"

"Yeah, baby boy, I'm good! Let's get it poppin'!"

Curtis walked into the bar room to get us a drank. I stood there trying to figure out how I needed to handle this shit. My best friend was in love with the only woman I'd ever felt like I could spend the rest of my life with. The shit felt just like a damn curse! I knew Shelly had to be wondering what I was thinking, because it was obvious we had a serious problem.

As I stood in pain, my phone vibrated. To my delight, it was Shelly. The text asked for me to meet her in the upstairs bathroom.

I left the room and went up the stairs. I couldn't help but wonder if Shelly and my boys were playing a joke on me for the way I had acted toward Shelly while in LA, but they had never met her. They only knew what I had told Curtis about her.

When I got to the bathroom, I knocked to make sure she was inside. I peeked in, and there was Shelly, sitting on the bathtub crying. I knew then that this was no prank. This nightmare was indeed my life.

"Shelly, you okay, baby?"

She stood up and grabbed tight around my neck. "Jay, I promise I didn't know. I knew he had friends, but he never went into detail about you or Curtis."

"I know, Shelly, but listen. There is nothing we can do about the past. The question is, what are we to do now?" I turned away in anger with my hands on my head. "Damn! Why did you tell him your name was Michelle instead of Shelly, anyway, baby?"

"I don't know. I don't know."

"Well, you and I know that you can't date us both."

"Jay, I like Shaw. He's really sweet, but I'm crazy about you! The way you make me feel, baby!"

"Shelly, this is my best friend. I can't just act like everything is cool and we dating the same woman. He and I both have some deep feelings for you, Shelly."

"I know, Jay, but I don't know what I'm supposed to do. This is a crazy situation for all three of us."

"Shelly, I can't just sit back and watch my friend live happily ever after with the only woman that I feel should be my lady."

"I don't want you to just sit back either, Jay."

"Damn, this fucked up!" I was angry as hell. All I could think about is what I could have done differently the first night I met Shelly. "Shelly, I got to tell him what's going on, and we all need to sit and go over this like adults."

"No, Jay! I need some time to think things through." Shelly grabbed me and kissed me like she never had. "Trust me, Jay. This can only be between you and me."

"Man, I just don't want to hurt my boy. He's been through enough when it comes to stuff like this."

"I know, Jay, but if you tell him, it may result in us losing what we have."

I shook my head in disbelief and told Shelly we needed to get back to the party before someone noticed we were missing. Shelly returned to the party as I stayed to gather a few thoughts.

We had agreed to keep things a secret for now. At first I had a feeling that Shaw had seen me talking to Shelly the night we met at the club, and went after her to see if he could come up with a woman I had pursued. But Shaw wouldn't do anything that foul and neither would I. I just had so many thoughts going through my mind, 'cause you have to admit this was an unusual place to be.

I went back downstairs and joined everyone to bring the New Year in. It was extremely hard to act like everything was all good, but after a few drinks and dancing, I felt a little better. I can remember getting drunker than I ever have in my life that night. I guess I was trying to wash away the fact that my best friend was in love with the girl of my dreams.

Daylight came and I awoke at Shaw's place. It had to have been around eight thirty in the morning. I had a terrible headache, but I keep some BC Powder with me, so I took one straight up with a glass of melted ice. I didn't even want to know if Shelly was still there, so I headed for the door. Struggling to gather myself, I made it to my car.

Thinking, "What am I going to do about this shit?", I called Curtis to find out where he was and if he was going to ride home with me. He was good. Shit, some chick answered his phone and told me he was in the shower and that she would bring him home. Despite all the controversy surrounding that night, I couldn't do anything but smile at the fact that my boy had a night he probably would never forget.

On the way home, I hoped for a call from Shelly, but she didn't call. All I could do was wait until she did. When I pulled up at my place, Shelly's car wasn't there, so there was no telling what that meant.

All I wanted to do was take a shower and get some rest. I started to think that maybe if I just avoided her, then the feelings I had for her would just go away. At the time, that sounded like the right and only thing to do.

I felt like I should have talked to Shelly first before I played dodge ball, but I didn't do it. Therefore, the games began. I must admit the first few days were really rough, missing her the way I did. Not to mention how living right next door to one another made it that much harder.

About three weeks after the party, I decided to get out and do something besides think of my baby. After cleaning up around the house, I got dressed, took a shot of Grey Goose, and headed for the door. Right before I started out the door, I stopped to search for my car keys, and from Shelly's place I heard laughter. I knew it was her, so I waited, because I didn't know if she was with someone or on the phone. I heard footsteps and peeped out my door. She was all alone.

I exhaled in relief as she walked farther down the hallway. I felt like it was safe to step out of my doorway, and I did just that. As I walked carefully behind her, I admired that sexy walk she had, thinking to myself, "Man, look at that ass! Damn, I miss tapping that! The hell with this shit, I'm about to stop her right now. Shit, that's my damn woman."

Right as I started to call her name, she stopped! She was looking down into her purse, and I figured she might have forgotten something. Then, all of a sudden, she turned around. Startled, she looked up right into my eyes.

"Jay!"

"Hello, Shelly."

We both kind of stood there speechless. Then she came closer. "How have you been, Jay?"

"I've been pretty good. How about you?"

"I've been okay. Missing you."

"Why haven't I heard from you, Shelly?"

"Baby, I was so afraid you were upset with me, I didn't want to face the fact that we were no more."

"Well, to be honest, Shelly, I was trying to give you some space to see what you really wanted."

"Jay, I've been spending a lot of time with Shaw since we last talked. But, baby, he is just not you, and I want to tell him that I'm not feeling him like that."

"Well, why haven't you, Shelly? The sooner the better. That may be our way to ease our situation into the mix."

"Jay, he wants to be around me all the time, and he spends so much money on me. I tell him not to, but it's like he tries too hard to show the way he feels for me."

"Damn, my guy has it bad! I need to think of a way to get closer to the way he feels about Shelly," I thought as we stood in the hallway together. Aloud, I said, "Come here baby!" I grabbed her and held her in my arms as tightly as I could. "I missed you so much, baby, I can't help myself."

"I missed you too, Jay." Shelly laughed in relief as she hugged me like never before. "Jay, it feels so good to be in your arms again. What we gonna do, baby?"

"I know what we need to do. Let's plan a getaway down in South Beach. We can stay as long as you want, just me and you, Shelly."

"Let's go then, Jay. I'm ready right now." Shelly's face lit up like the skies on the Fourth of July.

"Cool. But first I want to spend some time with Shaw, to see where his mind is with your relationship with him."

CHAPTER 9

"Listen, baby, I'm about to go back to my place, call him up, and see if he has a little time to hang out with his boy. I'll call you later and let you know how things went."

"Okay, baby, but when are we leaving for South Beach?"

"Give me a day or so, and I'll let you know."

"Okay, Jay. Oh, and Jay?"

"Yeah, baby?"

"I love you."

Right when she said that, I knew I was in too deep. We gave one another a long and well-awaited kiss that we both wanted and needed.

We went our separate ways at that moment. It was time for me to face my friend and see how far gone he was over my lady. I hadn't talked to Shaw since his party, so it kind of felt odd calling him up out the blue like this. We used to talk on an every-other-day basis.

Instead of calling from the house, I decided to hop in my ride and hit him up on the way over to his place. As I was driving down Fourth Street, my phone started ringing. And, strange but true, it was Shaw. I took a deep breath and answered his call. "What's up, playboy? You been hiding from me, ain't it?"

"Naw, Jay, I been having a lot going on, dude."

"I hear you. Me too, home boy. What you 'bout to get into?"

"Shit, Jay, I need to holla at you about something, man. You got a minute?"

"Yeah, man, I was just about to give you a call to see what you had going on. You want me to head your way, dude?"

"Yeah, that's straight. Meet me on the back patio; use your key to get in, pimp."

"Okay, Shaw, I'll see you in a few."

On the way to Shaw's place, I grabbed a six-pack so we could chill and drink. I finally pulled up at my boy's crib, and like he had asked, I let myself in with my key. Curtis and I had both had keys to Shaw's place ever since he was married. We checked on his family from time to time when they were alive.

I walked through his place, and it looked like he had been having some long nights. Shaw was a pretty neat guy usually, but it was sort of messy throughout the place. As I got closer, I could see him standing on the patio with his hands on the railing, looking out into city.

"What's up, Shaw?"

"Aw, what's going on, Jay?"

"You want a beer, dude?" I asked as I studied his actions.

"Yeah, man, let me have one?"

"What's on your mind, dude?"

Shaw opened his beer and took a few big swallows. "Damn, this beer cold, just like I like it! Jay, you remember Michelle, right?"

"Yeah, the chick you met a few months ago, right?"

"Yeah, man. I've been having these bad thoughts about her, man."

"What kind of bad thoughts, Shaw?"

"Jay, I love this girl, man, and I'm sure she feels the same way, but I can't help but feel like she's seeing someone else, dude."

"Damn, Shaw, you just met the girl, man. Ain't no telling how many people she sees besides you, pimp."

I could tell by the look on Shaw's face that he was deeply in love with Shelly already. Shit, she had me under her little spell as well, so in a way I could feel some of his pain. But it was different with Shaw; it seemed as if he had lost his way, like he was about to do something crazy.

"Shaw, look, man, you just met this damn woman and you talking about you love her. Shit, it can't be that serious, dude."

"Jay, you don't understand, man. I'm not like you. I am a one-woman man! This girl makes me feel so good about life, man! Well, at least she did at first."

"What do you mean, 'at first'?"

"I mean in the beginning, it was like we could stand the test of time, and now it's like someone else has her attention."

"Damn, Shaw, what do you want from her?"

"Jay, you know I've wanted to start a new family since I lost Kay and my baby girl Harmony."

"I know, man. But, Shaw, it took you and Kay five years to tie the knot. You haven't known Michelle five months yet, and you ready to get married?"

"Man, Jay, I can't lie. I'm in love with this woman, dude. I have never had a girl this fine before, and besides, she's so fun to be around."

I knew exactly what he meant. As I looked at my friend, I wanted to tell him everything about Shelly and me: how I really met her first, but on the same night, and how much we cared for one another.

Shaw sat there slouched down in his chair, staring into space, looking, feeling, and sounding hopeless. "Jay, what should I do, man?"

"Look, Shaw, man, first you got to get a grip, player! You young, good looking, and got plenty of paper. If this chick doesn't want to do right, man, find someone else!"

Shaw responded in a defensive manner, "I can have any woman I want, Jay! The thing of it is, I don't want any woman, I want Michelle."

"Tell you what, Shaw, why don't you get out and test the waters? See what other fish are in the sea. After that, if you are still feeling Shelly like that, then let her know how much she means to you."

Shaw had this look on his face that I'd never seen, and at that time I didn't pay much attention to it. He calmly replied, "Yeah, Jay, you right. Thanks, man. You don't know how much you've helped clear my mind, dude."

I gave Shaw a man-hug and finished the last of my beer. "Well, Shaw, I got to get out of here, man, and handle a little business. I think I might have to fly out to Miami for a few weeks. You want to come, playboy?"

"Naw, Jay, I'm cool."

"All right, don't say I didn't ask! I'll see you later, Shaw. Hold it down, baby!"

As I began to walk out the door, Shaw said, "Hey, Jay! What happened to that girl of yours that Curtis was telling me you have?"

"Aw, man, I don't know. She stopped calling, so you know me. I ain't with chasing behind them; I just find a new one."

"Yeah, I know how you do it, Jay. Holla at me later on, and thanks for the talk."

Now for some reason after those last few words we spoke to each other, I felt really strange. Other than lying to my friend and pretending I didn't know what was going on between him and

Shelly, something else bugged the shit out of me. It felt like I'd forgotten to tell him something. That's not to mention the look he gave me before I left. It's funny how I could see this thing we had going bad right before my eyes, but I did nothing to right this wrong.

CHAPTER 10

After I got in my car and drove off, I realized what had me so uneasy. I had made the mistake of calling Michelle "Shelly" in the presence of Shaw. That probably explained the look he gave me. In a way, I kind of thought it wouldn't make a difference, that he didn't pick up on it.

All I really wanted was to get Shelly and get the hell out of sight for a while. So I called her to let her know how things had gone with Shaw and how I thought he felt. As expected, she felt bad, because she never meant to hurt him—or me, for that matter. I convinced her not to worry and that everything would be just fine.

She seemed so happy about our position when I hung up the phone. She looked forward to spending some time away from Memphis, and so did I. It was almost like a weight had been lifted off her shoulders, thinking that I had made everything right with Shaw, but I still felt haunted, worried, and dishonest. I hoped the trip to Miami would make things better and somehow erase the fact that I was in love with the same lady as my friend.

As I pulled up to my crib, I could see Shelly standing in the hallway window. Shit, it felt like my heart skipped a few beats. I could barely get up the stairs as she ran to me, kissing me like we were newlyweds. I can't even front, I loved every moment of it. I had missed her so bad from the time we spent apart up until I drove home from Shaw's place.

"Hey, Jay, I'm packed and ready to fly down to Miami!"

"Slow down, roadrunner. We won't be taking flight until the morning, but we still have the rest of the day to be together."

For the rest of the day, Shelly and I lay around her crib acting like love birds: playing with each other's feet, reminiscing about college, and listening to songs from the 90s. I can't lie; I was getting real used to being in Shelly's presence. This thing we had felt so right and unlimited. The more time we spent together that night, the less I felt guilty about not telling Shaw.

After a few hours of fooling around, I decided to make some dinner. "Shelly, are you hungry, baby?"

"Yeah, babe. I got a taste for some steak and pasta," Shelly answered as she lay on the sofa, watching TV.

"I tell you what: find us a good movie to watch, and I'll hook up something right quick. Shit, I'm hungry myself!" I marinated a few eight-ounce steaks, made some garlic bread, and grabbed some extras to prepare a pasta salad. Then I got some dinner wine then hooked up some twice baked potatoes. I set the table, and we sat down to eat.

"Jay, this is really beautiful, and it smells so good! I didn't know you could cook like this."

"Yeah, I don't own a restaurant like my boy Shaw, but I can do a little something."

Shelly and I sat at the table and enjoyed the meal. I cleared the dishes, then Shelly wanted to watch a movie.

"Jay, I wanna watch *Death at a Funeral*. Have you ever seen it?"

"Yeah, it's a trip. Go ahead and put it in, we can watch it again."

"Okay. Hurry up and come out the kitchen so we can watch it, babe."

I finished up in the kitchen and joined Shelly on the sofa to watch the movie. About twenty minutes into the movie, I noticed Shelly getting sleepy. I waited patiently until she fell asleep. I knew I would be away for a while with Shelly in South Beach, so I figured this would be a good time to call my guy Curtis.

I dialed him up, and his phone rang three times. Then he answered. "Jay! What up, baby boy?"

"Yo, Curtis. Check this out, man; I need you to keep an eye on my boy Shaw, man."

"Why? What's going on, Jay?"

"Man, I can't explain things right now. I'm taking off for Miami in the morning, dude, and

Shaw's a little down and out about that chick he's dating."

"Yeah, I know. Jay, he called me last night and asked me if I had ever seen your girl before. Jay, what the fuck is going on, man?"

"Curtis, trust me, man, you will never guess. I'll fill you in when I get back from South Beach."

"Man, Jay, I hope you ain't done shit, man."

"Naw, man. Well, look, Curtis, just keep this between you and me until I get back in town."

"Cool, Jay, but holla at me after you get straight."

"Bet! I gotta go, player. I'll call you up later." I hung up with Curtis, got back on the sofa with my baby, and hoped everything would blow over.

Shelly must have been pretty tired, because she was snoring her ass off. It was kind of hard for me to sleep like I needed. I kept dozing on and off. Finally as I began to nod off good, Shelly's text message went off!

One rule that I've always lived by is never go through your woman's phone. However, I did pick it up to check the sender's name. I had a gut feeling it was Shaw, and sure as hell is hot, it was my boy. It would have been fucked up if I had read it. I knew how he must have been feeling when he texted her, so I didn't disrespect my boy like that. I laid her phone back down and tried to get some sleep.

When night had passed, it was time for us to get away, just the two of us. Shelly was already up and having a shower. I got off the sofa to look out the balcony window.

"Jay, can you make some coffee, baby, please?" Shelly screamed from the bathroom.

"Yeah, baby, I got it."

Miami is a very sexy city, and I couldn't wait to get down there with Shelly. As I walked into the kitchen and began to make a pot of coffee, I took a deep breath and decided that everything would be fine. Shelly got out the shower and walked into the kitchen, wrapped in a bath towel. She was a slight bit wet; her body was glossy and smelled like body wash.

"Good morning, Jay," Shelly said in a soft tone as she put her arms around my neck.

I replied, "Good morning, baby! You look so beautiful, Shelly, you know that?"

We kissed, and she told me, "I can't wait to get away with you, baby. We're going to have so much romantic fun."

I then got a text confirmation that our flight would be on time. At that moment, I got a slight case of the bubble guts, because I knew from that point on, nothing would be the same.

CHAPTER 11

"Okay, baby, you go ahead and get dressed. I have to pick a few things up from my place."

"Okay, Jay, but don't take too long. It's only going to take me a few minutes to get ready."

I responded, "Yeah, right!"

"'Yeah, right' my foot, I packed two days ago!" Shelly screamed. She threw an ice cube at me as I left her place.

I began to think, "Shit, this might be just what we need. Maybe I can hook Shaw up with someone else and he'll forget all about Shelly."

I finished packing and headed back to my baby's place. As I came through the door, I yelled, "Baby, we got about ninety-five minutes before our flight takes off. Are you ready?"

"Yeah, boo, just let me check behind myself and we will be good to go, baby!" Shelly answered as she fumbled around the house.

"Well, look. baby, I'm going to grab your shoe bag and head downstairs. My driver is taking us to the airport, looks like he just pulled up."

"Okay, Jay. I'll be down in two minutes," Shelly said as she kissed me on the cheek.

I went ahead downstairs to load our things. While I waited on Shelly, I took advantage of the bar I had in the limo and made a tropical Hennessy, which is Hennessy cognac with a splash of cranberry juice, tonic, and pineapple juice, plus a slice of lime. I figured Shelly would want something as well, so I made her an apple martini.

Shelly finally came downstairs. As she slammed the door, she took a deep breath. "Sorry, baby. I'm ready! Let's go. Ooh, baby, is this my apple martini?"

"Yeah, baby, I'm getting you ready for the South Beach treatment."

"Jay, we gon' have so much fun!"

"Yes, we are. I just hope you can keep up!"

"Naw, I hope you can keep up!" Shelly said as she kicked back, crossed her legs, and sipped her drink.

We made it to the airport on time and our flight was right on schedule. The flight from Memphis to Miami was only about two hours and thirty minutes, so it wasn't hard to entertain Shelly on the plane. I let her watch a movie on my laptop while I did some searching in *Forbes* magazine. I knew that I wanted to be with Shelly from here on out, and the thought of relocating crossed my mind.

I had my boy Izzy at Bravo Luxury Rentals to meet us at the Miami airport. I always rented me something sexy to drive when in Miami, and my boy Izzy knew how to match my fly. "Yo, Jay! What's up, homie?" Izzy asked in his Cuban accent as we shook hands. "Jay, check it out, man. I got you something to roll in that I know you going to love, my man!" Izzy was excited. "Check it out, man. 2009 Rolls Royce drop head cabriolet!"

"Damn, Izzy, this a sharp mother-sucker right here!"

"Jay, this how we rolling while we in South Beach!"

Shelly screamed, full of surprise.

"Jay, you like it, homes?" Izzy asked.

Damn right I liked it, and so did Shelly. It was snow white with a soft, salmon-colored leather interior, and the top dropped. "Izzy, you know how to keep me on point, my man."

Izzy and I went over the rental agreement, and after signing off on everything, it was time to ride off in this beautiful car. "Jay, are you going to let me drive, baby? Please!" Shelly begged as she batted her pretty eyes.

I looked over at her from under my shades. "Yeah, baby, I'll let you drive later." The top was dropped on the ride, my baby was on the passenger side, and we were in Miami.

I couldn't wait to have some fun in the sun. I wanted to make sure our stay was low key, and at the same time embrace the atmosphere of the South Beach strip. I had the perfect place for our stay: the Stand. It was a nice hotel stay located right on the strip, at the center of all the action. Normally I stayed at the luxurious Fontainebleau

Miami, but since Shelly was joining me, I figured the Strand would be sexy enough for the cause. On top of my current situation, I had been banging the front desk manager at Fontainebleau, so that could have caused a bit of fuss. Like I was saying, the Strand was very sexy and the staff was fantastic.

CHAPTER 12

"Good evening, Mr. Thomas. Welcome back to the Strand."

"Thanks, Juan!" I answered the front-desk manager as I smiled at Shelly. "Yo, Juan, make sure Bobby takes care of our things. We should be back in an hour or so."

"No problemo, Senor Thomas! Here's your keys, and leave everything else up to us." Juan and Bobby where two of the hotel's best staff members, so I also made sure they were taken good care of. Check-in time wasn't for another hour and forty minutes, but Juan activated my room and keys so that when housekeeping was done, we could just go straight to our room.

"Shelly, we are right on time for happy hour at the Atlantic Bar & Grill."

"Sounds good, baby. How far is it?"

"Oh, it's right outside the hotel, baby!"

As we walked to the restaurant, Shelly suggested another place. "Baby, let's go to that place that had the guy standing in front of it with the parrot on his shoulder."

At first I didn't know where she was talking about. So I answered,

"Where?"

"That place where that guy had the bird on his shoulder, and there was a girl standing next to him in some tight-ass peach and yellow tights."

I laughed. "Oh, yeah, you talking about the Tropical Café. I guess we can go there, but I must warn you, you may be asked to salsa by one of the dancers inside."

"That's cool, I just want to go there 'cause it seems so Miami!" Shelly screamed in excitement as we walked on down to the Tropical.

This also is one of my favorite places on South Beach. The staff is beautiful and the Latin atmosphere is really sexy! I knew Shelly would love it, but to be honest I was looking to be a bit more laid back upon arrival. After seeing how excited my baby was, though, I ended up feeling that good old party vibe that only South Beach could trigger.

When we got inside, the music was loud and sexy, and the people were dancing, drinking, and having fun. We ordered a few margaritas and some food, then indulged in the festivities. I knew this would be good for us because Shelly had never been down here before. We could be free as we wanted.

At least two hours passed before we knew it, but you know what they say about time flying when you are having fun. Shelly and I began to wind down and headed back to our hotel. As we started down Ocean Drive, I noticed a guy looking out of place and paying lots of attention to us. It really didn't bother me too much until I saw him get up and walk in our direction once we had gotten a good distance past him.

This guy could have been anybody for all I knew, but something just wasn't right about him.

Finally we were back at our hotel and proceeded to our room. Our suite was on the fourth floor with a beautiful view of the ocean.

"Wow, Jay, I love this place! It's so sexy, not to mention the view!" Shelly was very excited as she toured the room. I was a bit tipsy, so I flopped right down on the bed. Then Shelly yelled, "I know you not about to go to sleep on me, Jay!" She lay down on top of me and kissed me.

"Shit, baby, I got a nice buzz. I just need to take a quick power nap so I can be ready for later."

"Okay Jay, you get you a nap in, but you better make it up to me later!"

I turned the radio on just a bit so I wouldn't stay asleep. The radio tended to help me sleep and wake up, if you know what I mean. Shelly lay down with me, watching the television, but after a little while she went to sleep right on my chest. I would say we slept for around an hour before awakening.

"Shelly, wake up, baby! It's time to get into something."

Shelly rolled over and answered, "I'm up, baby. I was just resting my eyes for a little bit."

"Okay, well, I'm about to get in the shower. What do you want to do first, Shelly?"

"Well, I was hoping we could go down to the beach for a spell and then just ride around in our drop top!" Shelly jumped on my back as I was thumbing through my suitcase for some underclothes.

"Shit, Shelly, it's about seven. We may as well ride around. I can show you a couple of sights, then we can come back here and get dressed for some nightlife."

I continued to walk around the room with her on my back as she answered, "That sounds good to me, babe!"

Shelly and I got in the shower together and washed one another up. After getting dressed, we began our South Beach tour.

We were just about to get our ride from the valet attendant when I saw a local tour guide. "Hey, Roscoe! What's going on, amigo?"

"Hola, my friend, long time no see!" Roscoe replied.

"Hey, Shelly, let's take a boat tour with my guy Roscoe! He'll take us all over Miami and show where all the stars live!"

"Yeah, let's do that, Jay! Sounds great!"

I proceeded to talk to my boy Roscoe. It was right at quitting time for him, but he agreed to Shelly and me on a quick tour. We had to walk a few blocks to get to Roscoe's place of business in order to get transportation to his tour boat. It was a beautiful night, perfect for a walk or whatever you could think of to do with someone that you really care for and love. Roscoe''s driver picked us up and drove us to his cruise boat. What made this moment so sexy was that Shelly and I were the only ones on the boat.

The sky was calm and the ocean even calmer. As Roscoe showed us all the attractions, I noticed that Shelly was kind of deep in thought from time to time. I didn't ask if she was okay, because I knew she was, and I knew what was on her mind.

With my arm wrapped around her body and her head on my shoulder, Shelly looked up at me and said, "Jay, when we get back home, I think I'm going to tell Shaw everything. I know in my heart it's the right thing to do."

I looked Shelly in her eyes; she looked so happy that I didn't utter a word. I pulled her closer to me and kissed her on her forehead. That was the last conversation we had about Shaw.

The night began to fall as the sun set, and we had reached the end of the tour. Roscoe docked and shut things down on his boat. Once he was done, he offered to take us back to our hotel. We laughed and shared a few stories along the way. Roscoe is a funny guy by nature, man, so he really had Shelly tripping out. Since I had known Roscoe for around eight years, he had a moment or two to share with Shelly about me. Finally we pulled up at our hotel.

"Hey, Roscoe thanks for everything, man. We really enjoyed it."

"Jay, no problem, man. I enjoyed you both myself. Now it's time to go home to my fat-ass wife!" We all laughed, knowing he was only joking about his wife being fat.

I closed the door, and as he started to pull off, Shelly waved and yelled, "Bye, Roscoe!"

Roscoe winked at me while driving off and replied, "Bye, sweetness! You take care of my friend now!"

Shelly looked at me as we walked into the hotel. "Wow baby, that was so much fun! I can't wait until tonight! I want to go to the club Mansion, baby!" she screamed in excitement.

"That's cool, baby. I think tonight is celebrity guest night."

CHAPTER 13

Shelly flopped down on the bed in a bit of fatigue. I took my shirt off as I walked toward the minibar. "I'm about to fix me a drink, boo. You want one?"

"Yeah, babe, fix me one too!" Shelly replied as she rolled over on the bed and turned on the radio. "I think I'm going to wear that light-green dress I bought at the mall the other day, baby. What do you think?"

"You talking about the one with the back out?"

"Yeah, see, this one here!"

Shelly pulled the dress out and showed it to me. The dress was a Nicole Miller, and I must say it was a very sexy dress. When she put it up to her body, I slowly walked over to her and put my arms around her waist. "Shelly, I have enough money to be anywhere I wanna be, with anyone I want! But baby, I am sure I'm in the right place tonight and from here on. No matter what happens when we get back to Memphis, I want you to know you have my heart like only you can have it. I have looked into the eyes of many, many beautiful women, but none of them has made me surrender to my emotions like you, and I promise no one will separate me from this feeling."

Shelly then began to shed a few tears of joy and security. I could tell she felt like our togetherness was official. This was a fairy tale for us both, and I wasn't going to accept anything less than a storybook ending.

"Baby, promise me you will always protect me with your love as well as your heart," Shelly asked as she looked deep into my eyes.

"Listen, Shelly, I have searched all my years for what I have here with you right now, and I promise you will always be safe with me." Shelly smiled in relief and gave me a nice kiss as she suggested we get ready for the night. "Go on, baby, get your fine ass in the shower. I got to figure out what I'm wearing tonight."

"You not gonna join me, baby?" Shelly asked in a seductive manner. I simply winked my eye and continued to search for something fly to put on. After a few minutes, I got my gear together. Then there was only one thing left to do—paint the town with my baby! I had to make sure I had something to match Shelly's dress. I knew if I didn't, I probably wouldn't hear the end of it.

Shelly's dress was a soft, kiwi-green, stretch satin that really accented her hips. I decided to go with some nice designer jeans, a warm yellow French-cuff shirt, and a sage green vest. I must say we looked nice.

Well, the stage was set. Shelly and I caught the elevator to the lobby, and I asked her to wait until the valet came with the car before she went outside. I walked out to wait for the valet attendant. Boy, I could not wait until we made it to the club. I remember standing there thinking about how things would be once Shelly and I got deep into the swagger of South Beach.

The valet pulled up, and Shelly walked out to the car looking so intoxicating that I couldn't wait to set the night off. We pulled away in my beautiful drop-top and headed to the club Mansion.

It's funny how some things just catch your eye and some things you never see. Remember the guy I had seen earlier? As we pulled in front of the club to valet there, I got out smiling and feeling like a million bucks! I happened to glance across the street, and I could have sworn I saw the same guy! It was almost as if he saw me look at him, and he quickly turned his head, puffing on a cigarette. In a way it was creepy, or maybe I just needed to relax.

"Jay, you okay, baby? What's wrong? Looks like you saw a ghost or something, baby!"

I grabbed Shelly by the hand as we walked to the VIP entrance. "Naw, baby, I'm fine and couldn't be better. I just thought I saw a friend of mine, is all."

I gotta tell you, as I walked behind Shelly, I felt like I was dreaming. She was so beautiful and so full of life that I had to look into the star-filled skies and thank my father above for this woman. We were shown to our table as our bottle waitress went to get our champagne. The music was sexy and the club was packed!

"Jay, I'm ready to shake my apple bottom. It's off the chain in here!" Shelly yelled over the loud music while dancing in her seat. Shelly had this crazy way of being funny and cute at the same time; you couldn't help but have fun around her. She was having a blast, and I was getting my feel for the night. I took one shot of patron coming through the door so I could feel myself relaxed. I was in the club with my shades on, staring into the face of excitement. I was looking around for my waitress when I saw a distant friend of mine.

"Jay! What up, baby boy? I see you back down in Miami!"

"Cue, how you doing, man? And who is this beautiful lady you got with you?"

Cue then says to me, "Man, she really don't speak English, but she perfect other than!"

This Cue guy was a bigger player than myself, plus he lived in the fast lane. He was a millionaire, but he was one cool dude.

"Shelly, I'd like for you to meet a friend of mine. Cue, this is my lady Shelly. Shelly, meet my guy Cue."

"Damn, Jay. Shit, she looking like a keeper!"

I laughed as Shelly blushed innocently. We shared our section with them and partied all night long! The night brought plenty of excitement as we all embraced the South Beach nightlife. Cue and his non-English-speaking beauty left around one o'clock. I thought it would be a good idea for us all to get some breakfast, but Cue decided that he was going to fly to New York on his private jet. Oh, and he ended up leaving with two other chicks that he met that night.

It was close to two o'clock when I asked my baby if she was ready to leave. Of course she said no, but it was time, so I suggested we go.

CHAPTER 14

As we begin to leave the club, I grabbed Shelly by the hand. She stopped me before we took two steps. "Hold up, Jay. I got to take these heels off, my feet are killing!" She struggled to keep her balance as she took off one heel and then the other.

Laughing at her, I asked, "You wanna ride on my back? Come on, get on Big Daddy's back!" I stooped down so she could get on my back.

Shelly laughed and hopped aboard. "Woo! Jay, you better not let me fall in front of all these people!"

"Damn, hold up, baby. You gonna choke me. Shit!" We both laughed as we struggled out of the club. "Damn, baby, your ass is heavy!" I said with relief as I put her down in front of the club. We waited for the valet, and she began to put her heels back on. "Shit, baby. you can go ahead and leave them off, 'cause you ain't gonna need them when we get back to the suite!"

Shelly looked at me drunkenly. "Well, baby first we need to hit an IHOP or something, 'cause I hungry as a slave right about now!"

I laughed so hard looking at her facial expression. I was hungry myself.

"Shelly, you know we have a kitchen in the suite. I don't mind hooking you up a little something. Or do you just have a taste for an IHOP?"

Shelly was wasted! She had definitely had one too many drinks. She had been sitting down as we waited for the valet, but right as he pulled up, she got off of the bench in front of the club. "Woo, Jay, I think I have to throw up. baby!" She pulled her hair back with both of her hands, leaned over into the grass, and began to release all that she had eaten earlier.

I went over to comfort Shelly by rubbing on her back. "Jay, I'm so embarrassed!" she said as she continued to vomit.

One of the club's staff brought me a cold towel to give to Shelly. "No need to be embarrassed, baby. We had a good time, and I'm sure you're not the first person to throw up after drinking in the club, baby. At least we made it out of the club!" I said, laughing as Shelly did too. I grabbed her by the waist and escorted her to the car. "Are you okay, Shelly?"

"I think I need to lie down, Jay, 'cause my head is spinning like crazy!"

"That's cool. I mean, I'm a little beat myself." I tipped the valet, and we drove back to the hotel. It was only a couple blocks away, so I didn't see a need for a cab.

As we pulled up, Shelly was still a bit sick. So I got her a Sprite and an Alka-Seltzer to help make her feel a little better. Aside from her getting too drunk, it had been one of my most exciting nights in South Beach. Shelly had a ball herself. As we made our way to the room, all she could do was talk about how much fun she'd had.

She drank the Sprite and Alka-Seltzer, and I made us both a little breakfast just in case she regained her appetite. I peeped in the bedroom to tell Shelly I had made some breakfast, but she was passed out across the bed. I walked over and put her under the covers, then went back into the kitchen to get my eat on. Shortly after that, I joined her to get some sleep, thinking to myself, "Man, what a night."

I guess it had to be around eleven o'clock that morning when I rolled out of bed. Shelly was up and out on the balcony. "Good morning, sweetness."

"Oh, hey, Jay!"

I then asked, "How do you feel, babe?"

"I'm fine, baby!" Shelly turned to me with her bathrobe on and quietly said, "Come here, Jay." I walked over in my tank top and sagging jeans. "I'm so glad I'm with you, Jay! I know you gonna make me happy forever."

"Shit, baby, forever's a long time. I was thinking more like a few months."

Shelly wrestled me to the floor, and we both laughed. "Ouch! Shelly, you hurting me!"

"That's what you get, Jay! I'm 'bout to bite you on your chest!"

We continued to wrestle and play until I got a phone call. "Damn, who could this be, calling me at this time of morning?"

"It best not be some woman, I tell you that!" Shelly said playfully.

I got up to answer my phone on the dresser. "Hello?"

"Mr. Thomas! Mr. Thomas! We have a serious problem! You need to come to Ravish quick!"

"Wait a minute, calm down! Who is this?"

"It's Vanessa, Mr. Thomas. Ravish caught on fire this morning!"

"Caught fire? Was anyone hurt?"

Vanessa answered back frantically, "Yes, I think about six people from the mailroom. Mr. Thomas, I was so scared, I don't know what to do!"

"Okay, listen. Find Alex and tell him to handle all legal matters. I'm on my way! Vanessa, get yourself checked out, and thanks for calling. You did a great job, and I'll see you in a couple of hours."

I hung up the phone and said, "Damn, Shelly I gotta jet back to Memphis. Ravish has caught the fuck on fire!"

"Damn, baby! I'm going back with you!"

"Shelly, you don't have to. You can just wait until I get things under control!"

"I'm coming with you, baby!"

Shelly wouldn't take no for an answer, so as she got our things together, I made arrangements to get us back in town as soon as possible.

CHAPTER 15

I wondered how bad this could be, but I could somewhat tell that it wasn't too bad. At least no one had been killed. Needing to get back to Memphis as quick as possible, I phoned Cue to ask if he could arrange for his private jet to get us there. He arranged things with no problem as I knew he would.

We caught a cab to the airport, where my friend Cue's private jet was set to pick us up.

"Wow, Jay, I can't believe something like this could happen after all the fun we've had since we been here!" Shelly said to me on the way.

"Yeah, I still feel like this is a dream." As many wonders and thoughts roamed through my mind, I felt like this was a sign of some sort. I wasn't really fazed by the fire once I found out that no one was seriously hurt, but it felt like something much more was on the way.

We finally touched down in Memphis, and to my surprise, news cameras were awaiting. I instructed Shelly not to get off of the jet until I addressed the media. "Jay, why can't I just come with you?"

"Baby, have you forgotten about the fact that Shaw is my friend and he could be seeing this? Relax, baby. I'll call for my driver to come pick you up and drop you off when all the smoke has cleared—literally."

We laughed. Shelly reached over and grabbed me by the face as she kissed me and said, "I love you so much, Jay."

"I know you do, baby, and I love you too, but I need you to trust me on this. After I get things squared away at Ravish, we can enjoy a nice, candlelight dinner, some soft wine, a movie, and maybe some hot, naked sex?" As I spoke, I kissed her after every suggestion.

"Okay, Jay. I'll see you when you get home, baby."

"Okay, Shelly. Listen, don't worry. Everything will be just fine." I got off my jet and headed for the cameras to get this nightmare over with.

Like I'd promised Shelly, I called for my driver to pick her up and take her home. After all of the mayhem at the airport, I went to see the damage to Ravish. To my delight, it was true that no one had been seriously harmed. The damage to Ravish wasn't too bad either, so pretty much all was good. I called my boy Curtis to pick me up from the fire scene. Hell, I needed a drink with my friend after so much going on so fast. One thing about Curtis: he was always just a phone call away.

I had to square off a few more things before Curtis and I took off. My business manager Alex was more than prepared to get things resolved as soon as possible. After all, that was what I paid his ass for.

"Jay! What's going on, man? Is everything cool?"

I turned around to catch the voice in the crowd, and to my delight it was my guy Curtis. I then screamed to the officer controlling the barricade, "Yo, Officer, let him through, man. He with me, I'm the owner." The officers complied and let my guy inside with me. We gave one another the man-hug.

"Jay, everything good on this one, homie? I saw a glimpse of everything on the news, and then when you called, I was like, cool, my boy still good."

As I laughed and shook my head, I grabbed Curtis around the neck in a big-brother headlock. "Come on, player, let's go get a drink, man! That's what's up!"

"I guess I'm buying since you got so much going right now."

We smiled and walked off to get in Curtis' car. As we drove off, Curtis started a new conversation up. "are we going to Bracardee's, Jay? Or you wanna hit up something else?"

"Naw, man, we going to Bracardee's. I've called Al at the bar; he gon' have us a set-up once we get there."

Curtis went on to say, "So, Jay, I know your rendezvous was cut short with the fire and all that, but how was it down in South Beach, homie?"

"Man, you know how I open up when I go there, baby! It was beginning to be a classic vacation to remember until this, but we had a ball, player." I smiled and looked over at Curtis.

He replied, "Yo, Jay, you know you my homie, man. You the realest cat I know. I just wanna say, be careful with that girl, man. I just feel like this is moving in a strange direction. You feel me?"

"Yeah, I feel you, man, but you ain't got to worry about that. My relationship with her will take its course as far as that's concerned." I replied.

"Well, that's good to hear, Jay, but your boy Shaw ain't doing so well, man."

By this time, we'd pulled in at the spot for drinks. Curtis parked and turned his car off. He rubbed his hands over his face, sat back, and took a deep breath. "Man, Jay, on the real—your boy Shaw has lost it, player! I mean, he ain't shaved, he ain't been to work, and every time I go by to kick it with him, he always got this insane-ass grin on his face, man! Now this could be all in my head, but it seems like ever since you took off with your girl, him and his girl just fell apart!"

I looked at my boy and said sadly, "Naw, Curtis, it's not just in your head, pimp. Come on. Let's go get that drink, and I'll tell you what's going on."

We went inside, and I told Curtis everything from beginning to end. Not to mention we both got sloppy drunk in the process. After Curtis had heard it all, he said, "Jay, I promise you, after you left the club that night, I saw that chick all alone and I thought to myself, 'Boy, if Jay saw this bad-ass lady, I know he would have got on that!' Then, next thing you know, Shaw was doing his thang. And to be honest, I was a bit shocked that he got the number, because in a way she seemed like she wasn't digging him, pimp! Man, Jay, really, I think you did the right thing. I mean, what are the odds? It was an honest mistake."

We both went over everything that had gone wrong and things that could have made the night different, and in the end we both said fuck it, it was what it was. Curtis knew I would never do anything underhanded to him or Shaw, and vice versa.

After talking to my friend, I felt much better about things. I figured it would be just as easy to get Shaw to see things as everyone else did. Funny thing, 'cause as soon as that feeling made sense to me, Curtis took one more shot of cognac and said to me, "Jay, whatever you do, man—don't tell Shaw anything right now. I'm telling you, Jay, he ain't right!"

As I looked deep into Curtis' eyes, I knew I had to consider that it might not be time to talk to Shaw.

Curtis and I got up from the bar and walked out to his car. He took me home. As I got out of his car, I gave him a pound and said, "C, thanks for the talk, homeboy, and make sure you hit me up when you make it home, baby!"

""Aw, Jay, I won't be going home tonight, player. I'm headed over to my little lady's house!"

"You mean the chick you slept with on New Year's Eve, dude?"

He answered, "Damn right!"

"That's my boo right there." I laughed and shook my head.

"I hear you, playboy. Well, call me when you get there, then." I slapped the top of Curtis' car. He shifted into reverse, pointed at me, and rode off. I watched him until he got onto the main street.

Standing in the parking lot, I dialed up Shelly and headed toward her place. She picked up on the second ring, and before I could open my mouth, she screamed, "Hey, babeee! Where are you?"

"I'm coming up the walkway now, about to get on the elevator."

Shelly quickly hung the phone up and races to the elevator to greet me. As I got off the elevator, Shelly was standing there awaiting me. She jumped into my arms and wrapped her legs around my waist, kissing me and holding tightly to my neck.

I walked down the entire hallway attached to her until we got inside her apartment. "Baby, what took you so long to come home to me?" Shelly asked, kissing me repeatedly.

"I stopped at Bracardee's and had a few drinks with Curtis."

"Well, I'm so glad you are here now. I got you some warm bath water ready, and I picked out a good movie to cuddle up and watch tonight."

"Oh, really?" I asked in a surprised manner.

"Yes, really, and if you are really nice during the movie, I have a nice, sweet treat for you!"

"Sounds to me like a deal that I can't lose!" I began getting undressed as I walked to the bathroom. While I was in the tub soaking, Shelly made some snacks to help us enjoy the movie. I was a bit tired, so I stayed in the tub a little longer than usual. To be honest, I actually dozed off for a minute, but I awoke to Shelly laughing at something on television.

CHAPTER 16

I washed up and slipped into shorts and a t-shirt. I knew how the night would end anyway, so I didn't need to get fully dressed. It felt so right to be with my baby; needless to say, she took my mind completely off of everything that had taken place that day. We watched the movie, and what can I say? We had some hot, butt-naked sex to close the show.

When morning arrived, I awoke to a busy schedule. Shelly was extremely exhausted from the last few days, and I got out of bed cautiously so as not wake her. I needed to get some things squared away at Ravish after the fire and everything like that.

I figured Shelly would understand me leaving without waking her up, but I left her a cute little note just in case. It never hurts to cover your ass when it comes to your lady. It was maybe a little after eight o'clock when I took off, so I expected to hear from Shelly sometime after ten.

After a while, I got a bit concerned that I didn't hear from her like I thought. I thought maybe she had some things to do herself, but damn, it was almost noon and I still hadn't heard from Shelly. I checked my phone to make sure it wasn't turned off, and it indeed was on. I addressed my staff and told them to take an hour to get some air. I sat there in the conference room after everyone cleared out, trying to decide if I should call Shelly or just be patient and wait for her call.

I unbuttoned the top button of my business jacket and got up from the table. Stepping out into the hallway to get my thoughts together, I made the decision to wait for her call. Something just didn't feel right, though, and as soon as this feeling went through my body, my phone rang. It was Shelly. I began to smile in relief, but that all changed once I heard her voice.

"Jay, baby, I need you to come home right now." Shelly was crying and seemed very hurt.

"What do you mean, come home, baby? What's wrong? Why does it sound like you're crying, baby?"

"Jay, please . . . just come home, baby, please!"

"Shelly! Shelly! Hello?"

The called had ended. At that moment, I felt weak and helpless, something I had never felt from this heart of mine. I felt pain, and I felt confused by Shelly's distraught voice. I alerted my staff that I had an emergency and we needed to pick the meeting up first thing the next day. Then I rushed to my car, calling Shelly repeatedly and not getting an answer. The funny thing is I never considered calling the police or 911.

I didn't know what to expect as I sped through traffic nervously thinking of my little flower, my Shelly, who had come into my life as God had intended her to. My heart was pounding hard as I finally made it to her loft, not knowing what was going on.

I made it to her door and it was closed, but I could hear Shelly crying. I also heard a second voice. I turned into her protector as I had promised her. I wasn't about to let anything happen to my sweet flower, Shelly.

I opened the door and screamed her name. "Shelly, are you okay, baby? It's Jay!" I peeked inside and cautiously walked through her loft. I reached for my gun, but didn't have it. I always kept my heat except when I was with Shelly, and since I had stayed the night at her place, I was without it.

I paused. I could tell there had been a struggle, but why and with whom? I screamed for my baby once more, and then from out of the bedroom, I heard a man's voice. "Yeah, come on in here, motherfucker!"

I rushed to her bedroom to find Shelly lying face down on the floor with my best friend Shaw standing over her, holding a hand gun to her head as he yelled, "Yeah, bitch, get up on your knees so this trick can see your face!"

I stood there weighing our options. It was obvious Shaw had found out about us.

"Shaw, what's this, man? You know this can't go down like this, dog," I said in a calm and concerned manner. I looked into his eyes, and he was no longer the friend I'd known all my life. Shaw had lost it, and I had to find a way to make this right.

Shelly was on her knees, looking at me, trusting that I would save her.

"Shaw, man, I need you to look at me, man. You my family, man, I would never do anything to hurt you, man. So you got to know there's more to the story than you know. Take the gun away from Shelly's head and let's work this thing out."

Shaw was sweating heavily and could not be still.

"Come on, Shaw. this ain't you, man. Just give me the gun and let's talk. We're all together in this thing, baby, like always."

Shaw wiped the sweat and tears from his eyes and answered, "Naw, Jay . . . we ain't together on shit!" Moving side to side, the gun still at Shelly's head, he continued, "Jay, I was already suspicious of this bitch cheating, and when you came over trying to pick my fucking brain, I became more suspicious!"

"Shaw, man . . ."

"Shut the fuck up, nigga, and let me talk! Yeah, see, I hired a private eye to follow her, thanks to your little pep talk, Jay! See, I was going to do that anyway, because I knew she was fucking off! See, you made one mistake, Jay—coming over to my house and calling my woman Shelly! Yeah, you fucked up! Shelly, nigga? I thought your name was Michelle, bitch!"

Shaw reached back and hit Shelly right in the face with the gun. My blood raced through my body; I wanted to save my baby from this fucking nightmare.

"Get up, bitch! Get back on your knees!" Shaw grabbed his head and paced back and forward through the room, talking to himself. I thought it was a time to try and reach him, but he began talking once more. "Yeah, Jay, I knew it was you after that, so I had my guy take off for Miami. Yeah, see, you told me, Jay, that's where you was headed. Remember, bro'? I know the only time you go there is to pick up a chick or to sweep one off her feet. All I had to do is find out from Curtis where you were staying, big shot. And since you a loud motherfucker, it was easy for my guy to find you in a crowd."

I got dizzy thinking of that weekend, but remembered that guy I kept spotting around. That had been Shaw's guy. "Shaw, I need you to look at me and feel me when I say this. You need to take that fucking gun away from her head. Stop acting like a bitch and be a man."

Shaw turned to the dresser and grabbed an envelope. I looked at Shelly and whispered, "I got you, baby."

Shaw threw the envelope to me and said, "Acting like a bitch, huh? Open it up, home boy."

"Shaw, what the fuck is this proving?"

"Shut up and open the damn envelope, you fuck!"

I opened it up and inside were photos of Shelly and me kissing and having fun together. I looked at Shelly with a sense of concern. Then I looked back at Shaw.

"Yeah, Jay, this all the proof I needed to bring us together here for a purpose."

My heart started to pound. My body felt paralyzed. "Shaw, be a man, dog! Put the gun down, man." Tears ran down my face as I looked at Shelly. When she looked back into my eyes, so afraid, I felt defenseless.

"Be a man, Jay? Yeah, you right . . ." Shaw stepped back, biting his bottom lip, and pulled the hammer back on his gun. Pointing it at Shelly, he asked angrily, "You mean like this?"

Shelly was crying when she softly said to me, "Jay, please . . ."

Everything began to feel like slow motion, and then *bang*! Shaw released one gunshot into the back of Shelly's head, killing her.

I could barely breathe as I watched her lying lifeless right before my eyes. I fell to my knees, feeling like if I had just had three more seconds to react, she would still be alive.

I had nothing to live for at that moment. Every reason I had to live was lying in a puddle of blood.

Then Shaw screamed my name. "Aw, Jay, I forgot to tell you—fuck you, player!" I never looked up at him, but I heard another bang. Shaw had shot his best friend, Jay.

I'd never been murdered before, so I couldn't tell if I was dying, but I'd hoped so. Then maybe

I could catch up with Shelly so we could enter heaven together.

Shaw stood over both of our bodies, and the last thing I remembered from that night was one final gunshot. Shaw had taken his own life.

One night led to this, three people connected by one cause . . . love. I still have trouble understanding what is meant by the phrase, "Everything happens for a reason." You see, indeed I was shot, but I did not die. Sitting here in the hospital bed, reliving that moment with you all, I wish I had died. I don't know if Shelly's death was payback for me taking love for granted, or if Shaw's life ending was the price he paid for being my friend.

I'm set to be discharged from the hospital in about an hour, and I'm not sure what the days to come will bring. My life will be different now, and it will go on without the only woman I ever loved.

I can still hear her voice, her laugh, and I can still feel her soft body next to my masculine frame. I can still feel her heartbeat, as vivid as the smell of her skin. She gave me love and I cost her, her life in return. I still feel like I'm dreaming. But when I look out at the sun-filled sky, I say, "After all this, I now know if there is one, I am not the perfect player . . ."

The END

ABOUT THE AUTHOR

———

I've always had a passion for writing books, with hopes of one day becoming a filmmaker. Writing gives me peace of mind and helps me escape from everyday life. Writing also helps me develop a connection to my readers, sharing a part of my creative world as well as giving them a reason to laugh, smile, and cry just when they need it. Throughout my childhood growing up in Memphis, Tennessee, I always involved myself in things like acting and performing as a hip-hop, R&B artist. I enjoyed being able to see the satisfaction on people's faces when I had done my all to put on a great performance. When writing, I can almost feel the bond between the reader and myself, which gives me a stronger desire to take them beyond the action of reading my books, to actually make them feel like they are a part of my stories.

ABOUT THE BOOK

———◆———

Torn between love and friendship, Jay must make a choice that might be his last in this romantic thriller.

Love is forever. Time is not.